SHIFT
RACING SERIES

In Memory of
Ric Noyes
Racer, Grand Forks
Racing Hall of Fame
member, NASCAR fan
July 2024

FAST FIX

C. R. Fulton

D1649081

www.bakkenbooks.com

ISBN: 978-1-963915-05-01
Published by Bakken Books
For Worldwide Distribution
Printed in the USA

BAKKEN
BOOKS
www.bakkenbooks.com

- 1 -

Rain pounds my race car's hood. I cross my arms, looking out at the grandstands and track. They're empty, and if the rain keeps up, they'll stay that way.

My crew chief, Slate, jogs through the pits, holding his clipboard over his blond hair. Rain splashes off his shoulders as he runs up the semi-trailer ramp.

"Whew." A puddle forms beneath him. "We'll race, providing the rain stops within thirty minutes."

Gabe, our mechanic, mutters in Spanish, his glossy hair reflecting a lightning strike outside. It's hard to believe that not long ago, we were enemies.

He scowls at his phone. "Weather radar shows it moving off in twenty-five."

"The question is," Slate says, "do we run wet

tires or slicks?"

"We need wets or Logan will spin out," Gabe says, eyeing the water glistening on the asphalt.

I turn to look at 22, the late-model stock car I race for John Taylor. Its black, white, and red paint shimmers in the bright track lights.

"There's a strong wind. If that keeps up, the track will dry off mid race." Slate rubs his chin, his eyes calculating.

I've been looking forward to this race for weeks. The course at Southern National Motorsports is four tenths of a mile. It's got a 17 percent bank on the turns and 7 percent on the straightaway, so it's a fast track. Plus, at 250 laps, this will be good practice before we take on bigger races.

The rain peters out, and we stride forward to give 22 one last check. I wish there were more super late model races for 77 that were close to home, but I'm thankful to get on the track no matter what car I'm in.

"You've got the pole position from the heat race yesterday," Slate says as he checks the tire pressure. "But remember, taking the outside can force you to the back of the field. Stick to your racing line and keep your cool."

Soon I'm in 22, pulling on my helmet, ready to take on thirty-one other drivers for the $20,000 winner's purse. I sure wish Piper was here to watch me race. Maybe another day. My stomach flutters at the thought of my "tutor." Would I be able to concentrate with her pretty brown eyes on me? I laugh. Probably not.

"Hey." Slate leans on the window while Gabe rushes around 22, checking the camber for the fourth time. "This race will be wet to dry. The track will start wet, and you have to be easy on the brakes and acceleration. Pretend the car is made of glass. But when it dries off and we change tires, then you can drive hard and really use those banked turns."

I nod as the announcer's voice comes over the loudspeakers. "Start your engines!"

I reach forward, my finger hovering over the start switch. The other cars rev, and the roar of their engines vibrates the air. A smile curls my lips. This is what I live for. Part of me longs for 77 and his extra horsepower, but this race is just for stock cars.

I flick the switch.

As 22 thunders to life, I settle my hands at nine and three on the wheel. "Let's go, boy."

Today's pace car is a white truck. A wide plume of water sprays from his tires as we head out. After five pace laps, I'm gripping the chrome steering wheel like my life depends on it.

Because it does.

I force a slow breath, squinting through the rain-splattered windshield. Race cars don't have wipers, and the drivers at the back will be dealing with blinding spray.

The semi pulls off into pit row, and my pulse spikes as I set my foot down. Leaping forward in response, 22 slides into turn one.

"Easy!" I shout, fighting the urge to hook the wheel like normal to correct the fishtail. "You're made of glass . . ." I bump the steering and ease off the throttle. The pack behind me is having the same trouble.

Slate's voice is clear over the helmet radio. "If you want to finish first, first you have to finish. Three cars have piled up behind you already, Logan."

A caution flag snaps above, and I back off the accelerator after only half a lap. Not a great beginning for a long race.

Still, I'm thankful for the chance to regroup. Soon the green flag waves, and 22's nose holds a beautiful racing line around the course. I splash through a small puddle, but at this speed it feels like hitting a wall.

The more I accelerate, the more the track feels like ice. I hunch forward, tense, as I feel for the tires' response. Every lap, the blacktop is drying. That means we're all testing the limits and searching for more speed.

Out of the corner of my eye I see a blue car with 01 on its side slip forward next to me. I hold the line, refusing to give him space to go around. The puddle is just a wet spot now, but neither 01 nor I back off as we approach it.

His front fender shudders as we sweep through,

then twitches my way.

"Come on, man!" I shout as 01 crunches into my passenger side. Grimacing, I wrestle the steering wheel, swerving hard but managing to keep 22 on the track. "No!" The racer slides by, and I gun it, 22 roaring. *On second thought, I'm glad Piper wasn't here to see that.*

"Take it easy, Logan." Slate's not making a suggestion. I obey, nosing back to the wall in third place, only to discover how bad the spray is. The outlines of the bumpers ahead are barely visible.

"You've got a lot of race left, and you'll find an opening to move up."

I simmer in third, watching the track dry and urging more and more speed from 22.

Forty-five clean laps pass when the second-place car pulls off into the pits.

"He's getting slicks!" I shout, knowing he'll be far faster than me with the grip they provide.

"Don't pull in yet!" Slate urges. "Let this play out. The first to change into slicks has a ninety-nine percent chance of wrecking. When he does, we'll change under the caution flag and gain time back."

I shut my mouth. Slate's knowledge just might win this race. Another lap zips past, and I grimace as the racer with the slick tires roars out of pit row. Two laps later, he slips past the pack and roars up on my rear fender!

"Slate!" I shout.

"Hold on. The track is damp, and he can't hold that speed with slicks!"

Sure enough, the car spins out next to me. I tuck 22 closer to the wall, zipping past as his spin-out gains speed.

"Pull in now, Logan!" Slate shouts.

Pit road is right there! I veer off, heating up the brakes as the caution flag flies. As I lurch to a stop, a water bottle flies through the window, landing on my lap.

As 22 rocks to the left, I crack the bottle open and drain it, then pitch it over toward Team Taylor's trailer.

Slate and Gabe sprint around the car, holding tires and tools like weapons. The pits fill up fast as the other racers pull in.

"Let's go!" I slam the steering wheel, my foot hovering over the gas pedal.

"Oh, no," Slate groans. I twist to look out the window.

They slam the last slick tire onto 22, but it wobbles, the lugs refusing to line up.

"Rookie mistake!" Slate growls at himself, finally driving it home.

I look over as the first place car slams back to the ground with new tires, a team of four pit crew leaps back, and he takes off.

Now 22 rocks, and I put my foot to the floor, chasing him down.

I draft off his bumper as I test 22's grip. We're now at top speed for this track. The lights turn on, adding yet another change that forces me to adapt.

"Forty-nine laps left, Logan. Start looking for that opening." Slate's words push me forward, but the lead car blocks every effort to slide past.

Second place won't do. I clench my jaw, veering to the outside, 22 screaming as we take the turn at full speed. I pull even with the leader but can't advance.

"No, stay on the rail!" Slate yells.

I glance over, but the car is tight against the leader, leaving no room to slide in.

They hug the racing line, and I'm forced off. Lap by lap, that disadvantage sucks me back into the pack until I finally find an opening in fifth place and slide into line.

A frustrated growl expresses my passion.

"Twenty laps left," Slate says. "Anything can happen. Just keep your eyes open."

Then the third- and fourth-place cars bump together, smoke rising from their tires as they lock up. I swerve hard to the outside, and 22 shudders as we hook around the wreck.

The caution flag comes out again, allowing me to refocus. I'm in third place now, and I feel like I have a shot! At the green flag, we surge forward, the track so different from when we started.

"Watch this guy, Logan." I know Slate's talking about the second-place car. "He swung wide twice in the last fifteen laps at turn three. Chances are he'll do it again and give you a heartbeat to make a move."

"Right," I reply, holding tight to his bumper and doing 89 mph. On such a short track, it feels like 160. I hound the driver, lap after lap.

"Now!" Slate shouts, but the car hasn't shifted out of place. "Now!" he roars.

I shake my head, surging forward with no logical reason to do so. Time slows down as I rush straight toward his bumper, fingers crushing the steering wheel. Then, at the last millisecond, he swerves wide just off the racing line.

At last 22 is loose on the track, but I hook it tighter, demanding it stay straight, and I slide into second place.

"Fight for it!" Slate shouts as the driver tries to reclaim his place.

"No way!" I don't give him the chance, and he drops back, just like I did.

"Nice move." Slate's applause echoes through the radio.

"Yeah, but I'm still in second!" I shout, the veins in my neck standing out.

"Three laps left. Keep it right there, Logan." Slate's voice is deep and confident.

"What?" I cry.

"You heard me. Take the final turn wide with the hammer down. It's your only chance."

Sixteen seconds later I'm coming out of turn four, and I imagine the move, playing it over and over in my mind.

The white flag snaps above. This is it, lap 250. Everything else disappears—the massive grandstands, the pits, the rest of the pack. There's only the asphalt straight ahead.

The g-force pulls me far to the outside, my teeth

bared as I see the finish line after rounding the last corner. The lead car is to my left. Taking the turn wide paid off.

I ask 22 for everything he's got. He presses me back in the seat as we leap forward, bumper to bumper with the leader! We flash under the checkered flag, and the crowd is on its feet, cheering.

"Who won?" I ask as the car slows, every cell focused on Slate's response.

"Hold on. It's a photo finish!"

We sweep around the track, coming down to 20 mph. Exhaustion settles in.

Slate shouts, a wild cry that makes me flinch. "You took it, Logan! By a quarter of an inch! Whoo!"

I melt against the harness, pulling to a stop. My helmet clunks against the steering wheel. That race took a lot out of me. Even through my exhaustion, I can't help but wish that Piper actually was here. What a race!

Then Slate is there, slapping my shoulder through the window. Gabe runs his hand over 22's hood as if he's a racehorse. I know Gabe's tweaks gave 22 the power to gain first place.

A smile grows on my face as I pull myself out of the car. My tightly fitted black-and-yellow jumpsuit displays the Team Taylor colors, matching Slate's and Gabe's. We look like a real team now, and we won like one too.

Slate shakes his head as the announcer walks over with a huge trophy, then leans in, his words for Gabe and me alone. "You should have been twenty-one laps ahead after the second half. We have to fix our pit stops."

I nod, still flying high on the adrenaline rush. It's the closest race I've ever run.

The sun glints off 77's black hood as I sweep around the empty track. Today there are no other cars to battle, just a set of tires and a fuel tank.

I thunder around turn four on the short track at Carteret and slip into pit row. With a tire under each muscular arm, Slate is poised like an attacking leopard.

Gabe, my archenemy turned best mechanic ever, holds an air-powered lug wrench as he crouches forward. I brake hard, the super late model ready for its tenth tire change of the day.

As soon as I stop, I start the timer, watching seconds roll past. As 77 rocks to the left, Slate and Gabe rush around, jacking the car and changing tires.

John, the owner of Team Taylor, holds a fuel

tank over his shoulder, sweat rolling down his face. Slate, Gabe, and John leap back as the air hose is pulled clear.

I click the stopwatch: 24.8 seconds. I frown at the readout, then show it to Slate as I shut 77 down.

He hisses, running a hand through his sandy hair. Gabe mutters something in Spanish.

"The best NASCAR pit crews complete a full four-tire change and fuel up in 8.6 seconds," Slate says. "We can't compete."

John wipes his brow. For a millionaire team owner, he's proved more than willing to get his hands dirty. "We'll also need a ventilation system for Logan on the longer races because the heat can be brutal. I think we should put the money we won back into the team."

I nod, looking over at Gabe. I know his family could use the extra money if we split the earnings between us.

"Yeah, I'd like to put a new turbo on too," he says. His answer solidifies my newfound trust in him. A month ago, I couldn't have imagined us sharing the same goals.

John leans on the windowsill. "What about some ice packs for your race suit?"

"That'd be great," I say. It's happening! We're becoming a professional race team.

John and Slate are focused on one thing: become NASCAR material. My chief memory of the race is the heat. Everything runs hot on the track. The track itself can reach 180 degrees. The tires reach 210 degrees, and inside the car can get up to 140.

"We need more hands on the team," Slate says. "Fast hands. Two more guys would be great. Do you know that professional pit crews recruit star linebackers straight out of college?"

Gabe stretches and then winces. "Yeah, I can see why."

Slate grins. "That's why Team Taylor's instituting a new fitness routine."

Gabe's mouth falls open in shock. I can't contain a laugh. "You'll live, Gabe."

"Not so fast, Logan. You have to be at the top of your game, which means you'll need to outwork everyone else."

That wipes the smile off my face.

"If we're going to win, we have to live like winners. Tomorrow we jog, and the next day we lift weights."

Slate's not kidding around.

Gabe and I groan. That makes Slate way too happy. "Buckle up, boys. There's a lot to learn. Anybody know someone with fast hands who's willing to travel and work hard?"

Slate's question is greeted with complete silence. He sighs.

"I'm gonna burn off some steam," I say, pressing the start button and letting 77's massive power vibrate into my being.

The short track is nothing at all like a longer, steep-banked one. Here I can only use a fraction of 77's horsepower. But more than that, the bigger tracks require higher skill. I surge around, racing to stay ahead of all the pressure.

If we can't build a stellar pit crew, the winner's circle will never be mine.

- 2 -

I follow Gabe out of Slate's truck, and we stare at an asphalt go-kart track. It twists around, with tires lining the tight turns.

A cart zings by. It's wide, low, and fast. I laugh. It's been years since I was in a cart, and now I can't wait!

I slap Gabe's shoulder. "Ready?"

"If I was going to fix them, yeah. But I'm no driver."

Slate rubs his hands together. "This is a team-building exercise, boys. Let's work as a unit and build trust."

By the time we have our helmets on, it's hard to contain myself. The unique sound of go-kart engines starts a slow burn inside. With 212 CCs, they have enough power to do 35 miles per hour, maybe more if the driver knows how to get the most out of them.

I contort myself into one of the go-karts, nearly having to fold in half. But the harness creates an even deeper connection to the small machine than just a seatbelt. As a kid, I felt like I was plugging into the machine.

I rev the engine, then glance at Slate. His shoulders are wider than the cart frame, and he looks ridiculous in the tiny machine. With his knees smashed against his chest, I don't see him lasting very long.

"You're all set!" the attendant yells over the engines. Slate's cart leaps forward like a shotgun blast. I shake my head. So much for team building. Gabe's cart lurches forward, then stops. I'm thankful for the helmet that covers my grin.

"You got this!" I shout, easing up beside him. Soon we're cruising the course at quarter speed. The hairpin turns call me forward, and I'm longing to pit myself against the track.

Slate zips past, letting out a long whoop, the cart's engine maxed out. He must be doing at least

35 miles per hour.

Gabe gains speed next to me as we sweep around the first wide curve. The asphalt is just inches away, and the wind buffets my chest. It's so different from being inside 77. Slate goes past again, even faster, but I stick with Gabe. Teamwork is crucial for winning bigger races. I don't want to miss out on this opportunity to build trust.

Slate slows on the next lap, cruising next to us.

"Feel better?" I shout over the engines.

"Yeah!" he yells with a wild laugh. "Follow me!"

We string out behind him, zipping along as he leads us through the course. One thing is clear: Slate can drive, and he's determined to take Team Taylor to the top.

"Fun time's over," Slate says back at Burnout Bay as he watches a white Toyota Camry cruise slowly past.

I stare at a section of concrete barrier like a spectator at the Thruway. It's sitting near the edge of my driveway. "What's that for?"

"It's the same height as the pit barrier at most tracks. To speed up our times, we'll be leaping it while carrying two tires each," Slate says with a grin.

"Have fun with that," I say, pulling a soda from the fridge next to the toolboxes.

"Whoa, not so fast. Soda?" Slate can be super intimidating when he's got his hands on his hips like that. "Do you realize what that's doing to your body?"

"Um . . . It's tasting superb and hydrating me?" I say, enjoying the hiss of popping the can open.

"No, soda is actually *dehydrating*. Did you know your brain uses half the energy in your entire body? But soda floods your cells with so much glucose that it can shut down neurotransmitters in your brain."

"English?" I wrinkle my nose as I take a sip.

"That soda is messing with your brain. Slowing down your response times for hours after drinking it. Top drivers have the body of an Olympic athlete, the brain of a top-level chess player, and the reaction times of a cheetah. That soda will ruin all of that."

I hug the can to my chest with a frown.

"Hang on. He gets out of leaping the wall while carrying two ninety-pound tires?" Gabe asks, missing the intensity of the battle I'm in over the soda. He's holding two racing tires, one under each arm as sweat rolls down his face.

"No way. We *all* start with ten jumps today. Then we run a mile," Slate says.

Gabe and I moan. It's so hot I could toast a Pop-Tart on the driveway. But we're saved by an unfamiliar car pulling in the drive. A lady gets out, and I glance at the house, wondering if Mom saw the car pull in. My brief glance gives me the perfect opportunity to see Gabe's eyes go wide and his mouth fall open.

I turn to see what he's staring at. A blonde girl steps out of the car. Dressed in a jean skirt and a white top, she has a shy look as she stands next to her mom.

"Hello, I'm Jill Sanders, and this is Cindy," the woman says.

I elbow Gabe, and his mouth snaps closed as Mrs. Sanders continues. "We just moved in down the road."

Mom steps out with a bright smile, inviting them inside.

Gabe's eyes lock on the door.

"Cindy," I say, in a saucy tone.

Gabe drops the tires and clobbers my shoulder. I duck his next semi-friendly punch.

"Alright! Let's put this energy to use." Slate rolls two tires at me. Then he stoops to pick up a piece of trash blowing across the lawn. He reads the greasy wrapper. "Loco Taco?"

"Ugh." The tires are heavier than they look. We rush for the concrete, waddling like penguins as we struggle with the weight. It's next to impossible with those things. By the time we've done five leaps, we're panting like crazy.

Cindy and her mom are pulling out, giving them a clear view of our unusual training area. Gabe clears the wall, this time with ease.

"Hey, Slate, I have the solution!" I say. "Invite

Cindy to every race, and Gabe will complete an eight-second tire change all by himself."

I spin away as Gabe leaps for me. "See?"

- 3 -

"Mom, I'm going for a bike ride!"

Mom steps out of the bathroom, putting in an earring and giving me *the mom* look. "There's no airstrip racing on the other end of this bike ride, right?"

I sigh. I earned her comment by not telling her the complete truth last time. "No, I just need some time to think. The team won't be at Burnout Bay until noon to work on the cars. I'll be back by then."

"Honey," she turns to Dad, who's cinching his tie tighter, "what do you think?"

"Go ahead, Logan. Every man needs time to clear his head. I wish I had some." He bends to kiss Mom goodbye, and then he pats my shoulder. "See you tonight."

We watch him walk out the door.

"It must be a big case," I say. "This is his fifth day in a row in court."

Mom frowns, "At least it's not as big as the last one . . ." Then she clamps her mouth shut.

I squint at her. Experience tells me there's no way I'm going to get the info from her, but curiosity forces me ahead. "As in, the last case in Iowa?"

She turns into the kitchen without answering, which solidifies my theory that there's something about our move that they're not telling me, something about Dad's work.

"Did you eat?" she asks.

"Yeah, I'll see you, Mom."

As I pedal down the road, I slow near a white Toyota parked in the woods. It looks abandoned, but the wind stirs, and a food wrapper skitters under the car. I look both ways, then veer closer, the sand dragging on my wheels.

I stop and look inside the car. There's a blanket, a pair of binoculars, and a bag of Mexican food. It's just a few yards from my driveway. There's no reason anyone should park here. I shake my head and then set off, my current pit crew problems overtaking my mind again.

Soon it's just me and the salty air as I pedal toward Emerald Isle. It's not far to the causeway, the huge bridge that connects the mainland to Emerald Isle and its thin strip of beach filled with houses. A glimpse of the Atlantic Ocean reminds me of meeting John Taylor and of the first time I sat in a Ferrari. Her name was Sophia. I laugh out loud, drawing looks from the people gathered at a beach shop. Gabe and I forged a friendship inside that car too—as we beat it to smithereens.

Thinking about that day gives me hope. You never know what's waiting around the corner. And our team sure needs *something*. Or rather, some*one* with fast hands. It takes a lot of people to race a car.

I pedal harder, enjoying the fresh ocean breeze.

Something brown flashes in the corner of my eye. There's no time to react before it slams into my front wheel and I fly over the handlebars, stretched out like a seagull. My arms pinwheel, then I crash into the curb, my helmet slamming into a chain-link fence. I groan, certain I hit a dog. Did it survive? I look up, but all I see is a basketball rolling into the road.

A chorus of cries makes me glance over my shoulder. The fence I had tried to dismantle with my head surrounds a basketball court. A slew of boys are staring at me.

"Bro, you took him out!" one of them says, pointing at me.

"Yeah, man, that was crazy."

An older man rushes through the gate toward me. "Are you alright?" He reaches down, but I scramble to my feet, hating to look like a fool.

"Sure, I'm good."

"But you're bleeding." The man has brown hair with a tinge of gray at his temples.

I twist my arm, discovering a brush burn on my

elbow. "I've had worse."

Traffic grinds to a halt as the ball ricochets off a Mustang's tire.

"I'll be right back." The concerned man jogs out and snatches the basketball, waving an apology to the drivers.

"Do you need to see a doctor?" he asks when he returns, pulling my bike upright. The front wheel is bent, two spokes broken. "Looks like you might need a ride home."

I shrug, unclipping my helmet.

"Come on." He throws the ball back over the fence. The boys are on it in a heartbeat, returning to their game. "I think you should sit down for a minute."

I'm about to protest, pulling out my phone to call Mom for a ride, but a tall kid with shaggy blond hair steals the ball, twisting and feinting as if he's in fast-forward while the other guys are standing still. Then he shoots it, watching as it swishes.

"Whoa." My fingers hook into the fence as I watch him take another shot. It's as perfect as the last one.

Half the boys grumble while the others cheer. The kid has some fast hands.

"Maybe sitting would be good," I say.

"I'm Dave Demarco," the man replies, holding out a hand as we sit. I shake it, but my eyes lock on the game.

"Logan Reed. Who's that kid?" I ask, pointing.

The tall boy fakes out two opponents, then makes another clean shot.

Dave laughs. "That's Jaden Williams. He's got some moves, doesn't he?"

I nod, picturing him leaping the wall and zipping off tires at lightning speed.

"He's had a rough past, like most of these boys. But he's on the right road now." Dave whistles when a short boy makes a shot. "Nice, Brent!"

The easy connection between Dave and the boys is clear. A sheen of sweat on his face tells me he's normally on the court too.

"Does Jaden like cars?" I ask, regretting setting my elbow on my knee.

Dave shrugs. "B-ball has been his one genuine passion. He hasn't seen much outside Emerald Isle."

Dave checks his watch, then turns back to the court. "Ten more minutes!" He turns back to me. "We play every Saturday. You're welcome to come anytime."

"Oh, thank you, but I'm into a sport that's a

little . . . faster." I fill Dave in on the team and our current pickle.

"You're looking for a new pit crew member?" Dave tilts his head. "It would be an incredible opportunity for a young man like Jaden. He's got the speed for sure. Hey, Jaden!"

Jaden does a crossover dribble as if the ball were magnetized to his hands, then makes a shot before walking over.

"Hey man, you like cars?" I ask.

"So I get paid to change tires?" Jaden asks, smoothing the peach fuzz beard on his chin.

"If you're fast enough," Slate replies.

I watch from 77 as Gabe picks up the twenty-five-pound jack with a grimace. I feel the same way. Just gripping the wheel hurts because all my muscles are overworked. Slate has been relentless with this new fitness routine. At least I get to sit while Gabe pushes the jack under the car.

Jaden lofts the lug gun, frowning at it. "What's the catch?"

Dave said Jaden had a rough past, and his natural suspicion shows through.

"The catch is, you have to travel, work extremely hard, and put up with these two." Slate points at Gabe and me with a smile.

Jaden flicks the trigger, and the tool's familiar sound fills the air. *Zrrip, zzrip, zzrip.* Slate holds up a stopwatch. "Go!"

Gabe launches forward, sliding the jack under 77's side peg. The car tilts with one quick pump from the tool. The lug nuts fling away as Jaden uses the gun for the first time. Slate slams the stopwatch, staring at the readout. I don't need a clock to tell me that the change was fast. Way faster than Gabe or Slate can change lug nuts.

"Sorry, man, I can do better. Give me another shot." Jaden's still on his knees at my front tire.

I grin as I grip the wheel. With Jaden on the team, we might have a chance.

Slate hands me the stopwatch. "Put those lugs back on. We'll do a real pit stop this time. Logan, one lap."

I push the start button as Jaden zips the lugs tight and then wait for Gabe to lower 77. As soon as he does, I pull out like my tail is on fire.

Carteret's track feels so small after the longer tracks. I'm back in pit row in just seconds, roaring toward my team. That's a big part of what the pit crew needs: trusting the driver who's barreling toward them at 50 miles an hour to stop at the right place. I break hard and hit the stopwatch as I shut off 77.

Slate, Gabe, and Jaden rush forward. They get in each other's way, and the air hose tangles on the jack. Slate even drops a tire. But when 77 slams down with four fresh tires, the clock reads twenty seconds flat.

"Whoa!" Slate shouts. "Imagine what that will look like with some practice!"

"Like a winning team," I say with a smile.

"So who's your favorite racer?" Gabe asks Jaden.

"Oh, probably Usain Bolt."

Slate, Gabe, and I look at each other and then burst out laughing. At least he's got fast hands.

– 4 –

"Logan, you overshot the pit!" Slate's grumble is all too clear inside my helmet.

We all look good in our new matching helmets and jumpsuit with "Team Taylor" proudly displayed across the chest, but this is our thirty-first pit stop today, and at least one of us has messed up on every single one.

"Okay, let's take a break," Slate says with a sigh.

I crawl out of 77 and snatch a bottle of water from Slate. All I want is a soda.

"Listen up, boys. We have to work as a unit, with everybody in the right place at the right time. That takes trust. The car weighs thirty-five hundred pounds, and it's coming at us at almost fifty miles per hour. Each tire weighs ninety pounds, and they have to be under control at all times. We need to be a unit, with everybody in perfect rhythm. I think it's time for something . . . different."

My eyes go wide. Who knows what Slate has in mind?

"Tomorrow, bring your swim trunks," he says, running a hand through his hair.

The next day at school, I'm so sore I can barely keep up with the hallway traffic. I grimace as I lean against my locker. Gabe walks up, his gait as stiff as mine. Cindy Sanders breezes by, not even noticing us, but Gabe's red face tells me he didn't miss her sudden appearance. It's the first time I've seen her in school, and it's a relief to know Piper probably won't come between Gabe and me anymore. But still I battle nerves since Gabe and I haven't crossed his "you don't know me in school" boundary yet.

"Ouch," he says, straining for a last look at Cindy as he rubs his arm. "What do you think Slate has up his sleeve for today?"

I squint at him, needing to know the rules. "I can't say. So . . . it's cool to hang out here now?"

He fist bumps me, and we both cringe at the

motion. "Do me a favor and forget how stupid I used to be."

I laugh. "Sure thing, bruh."

"See you soon," he says, heading to class.

With two weeks of school left, freedom is staring me in the face. The singular problem I have with it ending for the year is Piper. I hate the thought of an entire summer without seeing her.

I chew on that problem as I slide into math class. Mrs. Morgan plays a video of a jet engine, then challenges us to write an equation to figure out how much thrust it creates.

By the time I get home, my brain feels fried. I grab a soda, looking over my shoulder for Slate, even though I'm standing in my own kitchen. It tastes so good, but after a sip, guilt ruins the moment, and I dump the rest down the sink. *I have to start taking everything Slate says seriously if we are going to make it to NASCAR.*

Soon Gabe, Jaden, and I are waiting in Burnout Bay, watching for Slate's pickup truck, dressed in our swim trunks with towels over our shoulders. When he pulls up, his truck is hitched to a beautiful boat.

"Sweet," Jaden says, climbing into the truck.

"How about a day off?" Slate asks, his button-

down shirt billowing in the air conditioning.

"Yes, sir!" I say, cringing at the movement as I settle into the seat.

By the time we get the boat in the water at Cedar Point Wildlife Ramp, I can't wait to jump in and escape the intense heat.

But Slate backs the craft out then throws the throttle forward, motoring through Brogue Inlet until we hit the open water of the Atlantic. The boat's bow tilts up, its motor roaring as we speed away from land. The ocean breeze cools us as we pass sandy islands, and soon there's nothing but blue choppy waves.

Slate stops, feeling at home there on the water.

Now I know where his tan comes from. Jaden proves to be the best fisherman, pulling up a mahi-mahi and three red snappers in quick succession while I wrestle in one drum fish.

Sweat builds, and I begin to think the ocean would feel good on my sore muscles. Slate sets his fishing pole in a rod holder and steps up next to me.

"Nice knowing you," he says with a mischievous grin. Then he pushes me over the rail.

The waves sparkle as I curl into a cannonball, my lifejacket popping me back to the surface like a cork. The cool embrace is refreshing, and I tread water, wondering how deep it is there and shaking my head at Slate's antics.

With a playful roar, he grabs Gabe's lifejacket, and the mechanic joins me in the Atlantic. Jaden proves difficult to catch even on the small boat, so it takes Slate a bit longer to grab him.

"Over you go!" Slate yells as Jaden's long arms flail. His shout is cut short as he goes under.

Gabe and I laugh, swimming closer to the boat. I cast a quick glance around for fins cutting the surface. Jaden bobs over, and we look up at Slate, realizing there's no easy way to get back in.

Slate tosses me a small device, then puts his

hands on his hips. I snatch the cylinder from the water, scowling at it. A green light flashes at one end, and "Personal Location Beacon" is written across the bottom.

"Listen up, team," Slate says with a tone that indicates we had better listen.

My stomach sinks to my toes as I stare up at him.

"You have to trust each other, work as a unit." He tosses random items overboard: an oar, a fire extinguisher, and three extra lifejackets.

"Let the ladder down," Gabe says, his voice cracking.

"Boys, if you're going to win on the track, you have to be a team off the track too. Today your job is to conquer one mile of open water to reach the Point at Emerald Isle. Logan, hook that beacon onto your life vest. I'll see you at the beach." With that he turns toward the wheel.

"Slate!" we scream together.

He turns back, and we laugh at his joke.

"Good one," Gabe says, stroking hard for the vessel, but his fingers find no grip on the slick hull.

"I almost forgot to leave you this," Slate says, pulling a white fiberglass cover off the motor. He tosses it overboard.

In that second, the fact that he's serious hits me, and I swim like mad for the boat, but there's no way to climb in!

"The tide is rolling in, which should help. Make sure you don't lose my things!" Slate says before he revs the engine and pulls away.

We bob in its white frothy wake, the blood draining from our faces as we watch his shirt billow in the wind.

"He's crazy!" Jaden squeaks, "He can't do this!"

Gabe joins Jaden's wild shouting.

I watch the boat getting smaller by the second, clutching my life vest where the neck of it presses against my chin. Then I clip the beacon on, double checking that it's secure.

"He left us!" Gabe continues in the same shell-shocked tone that I feel.

"Grab everything that's floating!" I yell over their protests, swimming toward the oar. Everything is spreading out, which makes my heart rate spike. The boat is a dot on the water now, and it's our only way to tell direction.

Gabe faces the fast-disappearing speck, treading water in the light swell. "Okay, when the sun is over my left shoulder, the shore is straight ahead."

"Yeah, but that will only last so long, until the sun changes position," Jaden says, scrambling onto the white piece of fiberglass, his chest heaving as he stares at the water.

"Shark!" he screeches, pointing at a shadow in the deep water between us.

- 5 -

Gabe and I swim like mad toward Jaden. We almost capsize the tiny piece of fiberglass. It has a covered foam backing that floats, but that doesn't help too much with three people trying to get on it at once. We finally scramble onto it and huddle together, searching the deep blue waves.

"There!" Gabe points at a darker patch that cuts through the water toward us.

We scramble away from it, and the fiberglass tilts, taking on water.

"Whoa!" I pull Jaden and Gabe back to the center, resettling as the shadow circles us.

A gray fin breaks the surface. Gabe slumps against me in relief. "It's just a dolphin. That's a good sign. They don't like sharks. They've even been known to kill them."

We all breathe easier, but the extra lifejackets are still floating away. The fire extinguisher bumps against our makeshift raft, and I snatch it up.

"Why on earth would he leave us that? What's the water going to do, catch on fire?" Jaden asks, his hair plastered to one side of his forehead.

"Slate always has a plan," I reply, blinking hard. "Everything he left, he did it for a reason." A wave makes a slurping sound as it splashes into our raft. I look toward the shore, determination rising. "Let's beat him to the beach," I say.

"How? He's on a boat," Gabe replies.

"Yeah, but he has to load the boat onto the trailer, then drive over to Emerald Isle. I say we're waiting for him when he gets there."

"Yeah!" Jaden adds.

"We need those life vests," I say, studying the situation. "If we flip this fiberglass over, it will move better, plus we could use the extra life vests to help it float."

One vest begins a wild zigzag pattern on the surface, then disappears.

"That is freaking me out!" Jaden says as the

vest pops into the air, then settles on the waves. A dolphin's head appears, its open mouth ringed with sharp teeth. A chattering sound fills the silence of the open ocean, then the dolphin drops below the surface.

I sigh. "We *need* those vests."

No matter how strange the test is, I'm determined not to fail. Slate said not to lose his things, and I don't intend to. Two deep breaths later, I dive into the sparkling water, a shiver of fear streaking up my spine. The dolphin doesn't make another appearance, and I drag the life vests back to the others, adrenaline pushing me forward.

"We have to flip it," I say, feeling more comfortable in the water.

Gabe studies the situation. "You're right." He frowns, then dives in next to me.

"Come on, Jaden," I say.

"No way, man. There are sharks in there. Legit."

I roll my eyes. "Flipping it is our only chance to reach shore and avoid being surrounded by sharks—or eaten."

Gabe nods in agreement as he treads water, checking his feet for nibblers.

Jaden hisses through his teeth then eases to the

edge of the fiberglass. Gabe and I share a look, knowing we could shove him off if we had to. But that wouldn't do much for building Team Taylor's trust.

"Listen," Gabe says. "It will only take a few seconds if we work together."

"I can't believe this," Jaden mutters. "I was supposed to be changing tires. How does stuff like this happen to me?" Then he proves just how fast he is as he slips over the edge. He breaks the surface like a submarine at full speed. "Go!"

We wrestle with the weight of the fiberglass as it tilts skyward, then falls in slow motion, flipping over. Jaden's back on it before it even settles.

I swim around and tie the life vests to its edges, tossing the fire extinguisher back on top.

"This *is* better," Jaden says, crouching inside the boat.

Gabe has the oar, and he reaches down, paddling until we're pointed toward shore as I climb aboard.

"Okay, we can use our weight to make this easier," Gabe says. "Logan, you shift forward. Jaden, come back a little."

We wobble into position, and the craft seems steadier. Gabe plunges the oar into the water, pulling hard.

I study the fire extinguisher, fingering the pull pin that releases the handle. "Motorboat, anyone?"

They look at me as I pull the pin. Shifting, I hold the nozzle underwater at the back of our makeshift boat and squeeze the handle. Bubbles and white froth disturb the surface of the water.

Gabe keeps paddling as we pick up speed. It sure feels good to be heading toward shore!

"Now we're talking!" Jaden pumps his fist, the sun glistening off his wet skin.

The fire extinguisher doesn't last long, but at least it makes us feel better. Gabe paddles until sweat is dripping from his elbows.

"My turn," I say, the boat tilting dangerously as we change positions.

"I can see land!" Jaden cries.

We all shout at the dark smudge. The sun is beating down on us, and my tongue is sticking to the roof of my mouth, but the thin strip of sand up ahead grows by the moment. Pelicans soar in formation, looking down at us with one eye at a time.

"My turn," Jaden says, and I couldn't be happier to hand him the oar.

His quick strokes set a good pace, and soon I can make out the almost deserted patch of beach they call "the Point." A chair sits on the white sand with an umbrella shading it. A wide-shouldered silhouette in swim trunks is sitting in the chair, sipping a drink.

"Slate," I mutter.

The surf proves a fierce enemy, and it's all we can do not to capsize. We close in on the shore by sheer determination.

"Move forward!" Gabe shouts as we almost tip over on the crest of a breaker. We scramble around as Jaden paddles even faster.

The scrunch of the hull on the sand sends a shiver of delight up my spine. A wave smashes us from behind, and we tumble onto the hot sand on our hands and knees.

"Well, he beat us to the beach," Gabe says as we stand up, watching Slate sip his icy drink.

"Yeah, but he's *way* too dry," I reply with a sinister smile.

Gabe and Jaden grin, and we trudge toward him. Slate raises his ever-present stopwatch. "A mile in twenty-four minutes. Not too bad, boys."

We glance at each other, then sprint forward with a roar. Slate's eyes go wide. He peels out of the chair, sand spraying beneath his feet.

I snatch his right arm as Gabe leaps onto his neck. Slate puts up a pretty good fight as the three of us drag him toward the surf. A wave finishes our wrestling match, engulfing us all. But Slate comes up laughing.

He tackles me, dunking me under a monster wave. When I scramble up, he's got Gabe under one arm and Jaden under the other. Then he tosses them in deeper. My frustration breaks, and I launch at him in pure fun.

Soon we're all sprawled across the sand, our chests heaving.

"Now, *that's* a team," Slate says, nodding as he looks out over the glittering ocean.

"What if we died out there?" Gabe asks, frowning.

Slate scoffs, waving a hand in dismissal. "I was watching your location like a hawk. Plus, the transmitter had a radio, so I could hear you the entire time."

A wave ripples up my legs as I sigh. "Next time we need to work together as a team, we'll just do it, no ocean involved."

Jaden nods. "You got that right."

"I agree," Gabe adds.

The sun sparkles on the water, and the oar

bumps on my foot. One thing is for sure: my crew chief is serious about winning.

Almost as serious as I am.

- 6 -

"So I talked to John," Slate says, his voice echoing in Burnout Bay.

I sit up straight, my eyes wide. Gabe rolls out from under 77 on a creeper, but Jaden keeps dribbling a basketball. He hasn't been around long enough to know that those words can change everything.

"And?" I ask.

Slate flips some papers on his clipboard. "He knows a guy on the West Coast who's got some tight connections with NASCAR."

My heart pounds at the mention of the word. "And?"

"He'd like us to come to LA for a meet and greet. Plus, he wants to see us on the track."

My mouth hangs open. Gabe flinches, falling off the creeper. Jaden stops dribbling.

"We're going to LA?" he says. "Sweet!"

"NASCAR?" I squeak, staring at 77, my head full of dreams.

Slate nods. "Except we're nowhere near ready."

His words are like a slap in the face.

"Our pit stop times are better, but they're nowhere near NASCAR material. Right now we're not even pro material."

I swallow a sour feeling as Slate continues. "You have a week left of school?"

"Five days!" Jaden cries, rejoicing. He's the only one of us who isn't feeling the stress.

Slate nods. "The race at Irwindale Speedway in LA is in two and a half weeks. It'll take four or five days to travel there, leaving us just one week to cut our pit stop times from twenty seconds down to ten."

Jaden snatches a lug gun, miming popping off lugs. "Going to LA? We got this, Slate, no cap."

"Gabe, what are your thoughts on the car? Is it ready?"

"Yeah, 77 is solid. 'Course, for this I could do more work."

"So, are we all on board then? This will mean the hardest work you've ever done and a level of excellence you've only dreamed of. All to impress a man who has the connections we need," Slate says, eyeing us.

"I'm in." There's no hesitation in my voice.

"Let's do it," Gabe nods.

"LA, yes!" Jaden dribbles the ball around his body so fast, it's a blur.

"When you know cars the way you know that ball, we'll be golden," Slate says. "Alright, boys, we've got a two-mile run today, then sprints to build up that speed."

Gabe whimpers, getting up. We stretch on the burnout marks as the sun blisters down.

"Let's push it today, knock a minute off our last mile," Slate says as he tightens his shoe.

"I'm not a race car," Gabe says. "I can't just up my horsepower." Running is as much his enemy as math is mine. He perks up though when he looks toward the road.

I turn and catch a glimpse of Cindy jogging past. Her long legs eat up the distance as she disappears beyond the house.

Gabe sets out, faster than I've ever seen him

run. "What are you all waiting for?" he calls back over his shoulder.

I laugh. Motivation is a powerful thing.

- 7 -

I close my locker for the last time this year. A B+ average across all of my classes was beyond my wildest dreams a few months ago. Academic achievement fills me with a deeper satisfaction than I expected, as if I've conquered a part of myself.

Piper leans next to me with a grin. "Last day, Logan!"

I let out a long breath. As much as I've longed for the freedom of summer, it means I'll have zero reason to see her. I've been attacking that problem from every angle, with no solutions.

"Yeah," I say.

She frowns. "I thought you'd be thrilled."

I open my mouth but shut it again before the

truth slips out. "You got any plans for summer?"

"Not really, just putting my new skateboard bearings to good use. Summer isn't my favorite season. Mom's not really . . . how do I say it? She's not *present* very much." Piper bites her lip, looking down. "Well, see you around, Logan."

My chest constricts. Where exactly is "around"? What she's really saying is, "See you next fall." And that makes my stomach clench. "Um . . ."

How stupid can I sound?

"Well, I have to catch the bus." She walks off, then turns back to look at me. This would be the perfect time to say something memorable, something life-changing, but all that comes out is, "Adios, Piper."

She waves and then glides away. I clunk my forehead against the locker.

"Did you lose a race that I'm not aware of?" Gabe's voice makes me stand up straight.

Despite his fast pace when Cindy was ahead of us, I dare not bring up the tender subject of Piper. I'm fairly certain his interest has landed solidly on Cindy, but it's not the sort of chance I want to take. "No, I just . . . It's nothing."

My heart twists, searching for a reason to call

Piper before she gets onto the bus, but the blank spot in my brain can't create one.

Gabe fist bumps me and then grins. "We better hurry. The *slave driver*—I mean Slate—wants more pit practice."

Jaden weaves through the crowded hallway toward us. It's amazing that we'd been in school together all year without noticing.

"Yo!" He leaps for the exit sign hanging from the ceiling, whacking it hard enough that it wobbles. "Dave is picking me up to celebrate."

"Celebrate what?" I ask.

"That I haven't dropped out like my parents or grandparents. We're grabbing burgers and shakes. I'm sure you all can come. He can drop us at your place for practice later."

I grin at Gabe. "Dare we keep Slate waiting?"

He shrugs. "I enjoy living on the edge. Besides, if all three of us are late, what's he going to do? Fire the entire team? Seriously, though, I'll just text him and let him know we'll be a little late."

Dave buys burgers and milkshakes for us all. I pass on the milkshake for a water. As much as it pains me, I have to start taking my diet seriously if I want to help Team Taylor get to the top. We jabber and joke all the way to my house. When we get there, Slate is backing the semi into my driveway. Dave pulls in behind him and puts the car into park.

"Yeah, I'm buying a dirt bike tomorrow, so I won't need rides anymore," Jaden says.

"Um, isn't it illegal for you to ride on the road?" Gabe asks.

"Who said anything about roads? I'll use the woods. My dad used to do that. I'd ride behind him, and we'd just disappear. Then *he* disappeared one day." Jaden shrugs as if it's no big deal. "You'll see, I'll be the ghost of Swansboro."

Dave laughs. "I'll keep the name in mind."

We pile out of the compact car, punching and wrestling. "Logan, can I have a second?" Dave asks.

"Yeah," I say, wondering if I'm in trouble as I follow him down the driveway.

"Listen, thank you for giving Jaden this chance. I can see good changes in him, and that means a lot to me."

"Sure thing, but we need him more than he needs us."

"Maybe it could be the opposite. Have you ever heard of a poem called 'Men and Trees'?"

I frown and then shake my head. "Nope."

"It highlights how trees rely on wind for their strength. The strongest wood comes from the trees that have withstood the biggest storms. People are like that too. The strongest of us have outlasted the storms of life, and we're better for it. Stronger. Jaden needs some fresh winds, some fresh challenges in his life so he can forget about the old ones."

I nod, thinking of our move. Those winds did make me stronger. "I hear you."

"You know, Logan, things worth doing don't have an express lane. It's a long road to achieve our goals in life." He pats my shoulder. "I'll see you around."

I nod, those words bringing back the problem of an entire summer with no Piper. As if on cue, my phone rings. I rush to look at the number. It's her!

Regaining my cool, I stride away from everyone. "Hey," I say, so glad my voice doesn't crack.

"Logan!" She sounds excited.

"What's up?" I ask, my heart pounding.

"Oh, I . . . well, how's summer going for you?"

I stumble for words. It's not like much of summer has passed. Did she miss me? Would it be okay to ask what she meant about her mom? Or would that cross some unspoken line?

Then my eyes go wide. She didn't have a good

reason to call? Is it possible she's been thinking of me as much as I've been thinking about her?

I clear my throat. "Well. . . uhh. . . I'm good. How about you?"

"Oh, I'm fine. I was just calling to see how you've been. . . ."

A rustle in the woods beside the house makes me scowl. A flash of a white shirt shows between the leaves. The hair on my arms stands on end. Why would someone be in there? "Piper? I'm sorry, but I gotta go."

"Sure. See you, Logan."

Part of me is flying high. She called me! Another part is outraged that whoever's been hanging around had to show up right then and interrupt the call. I zero in on the shape of a man rushing away.

"Hey!" I yell.

The figure streaks away. Before I can think, I'm running after him, leaping fallen logs and racing through the pines. Ahead, I hear an engine start. By the time I skid onto the sand near the road, I glimpse the white Camry pulling out. He fishtails down the road as I bend over to catch my breath. When I turn to go, something crinkles under my shoe—a Loco Taco wrapper.

Not long afterward, we're loaded up and on our way to Carteret Speedway.

The flags on top of the grandstands still make me shiver with excitement. I cruise 77 around the track to heat up the tires, so everything is as close to an actual race as possible.

"Alright, Logan, come in," Slate says over my helmet radio.

As 77 roars into pit row, Gabe and Jaden leap out in front of me. I'm still doing 30 mph, surging into just the right spot as they rush for the passenger side. I brake hard and click the stopwatch.

As soon as 77 tilts, the lug gun screams. I watch the seconds tick past. Slate slaps the fender when the crew is done, and I look at the watch.

Twenty-two seconds.

I sigh. Not impressive to a guy who knows NASCAR.

- 8 -

The next five days are a blur of pit stops. The guys have been counting footsteps, videoing themselves, and critiquing each movement.

Slate lets out a slow breath. "Okay, last one before we leave for LA."

I shiver just thinking of Irwindale Speedway. It's going to be tough to focus while knowing someone's watching, judging us.

I pull out of pit row. By now it's something I could do in my sleep. I whip around the short track and then cruise in. Team Taylor's like a machine now. The air hose snakes in front of 77 as I lurch to a stop, right on my marks.

I click the stopwatch, holding my breath until

the jack drops the car the second time.

"Fifteen point four seconds!" I shout, shutting 77 off.

"Yes!" Gabe yells, one fist jamming toward the sky.

Slate scratches his neck. "Didn't think I'd ever hear that. We got a shot, boys. Nice work. We'll leave at 5:30 tomorrow morning. Don't be late, or the bus will leave without you."

That night I barely sleep, my nerves on fire as I worry about everything that could go wrong. I'm staring at the alarm clock when it finally rolls to 5:00 a.m.

Downstairs I find Mom already cutting up a bowl of fruit.

"I'll just grab a doughnut," I say, scanning the fridge, which seems devoid of any actual food.

"There aren't any." She pushes the fruit tray toward me.

"Then a Pop-Tart will do."

She shakes her head. "Slate says no more sugary foods. They slow down your response times. And that means you can't drive as safely when you eat sugar. I wish I'd known that before."

I stare at her, still groggy in the dark of the early morning. "Mom . . ."

"Nope. He's right. You'll be better off if you give yourself good fuel to run on. Safer is always better."

I sigh, knowing it's pointless to argue with her about safety.

"Hey, Dad has a deposition in LA this weekend. He was going to send one of the other lawyers, but since you'll be there racing, we'll fly out and watch you."

"What? That's great!" It almost makes up for the lack of real food in the fridge. I grab the bowl of fruit and wolf down the apples first.

"Have a great time traveling with the team. We'll see you on Friday."

I hug her as I hear Slate start the semi outside.

"Love you." I rush into the garage, scooping up my bags, excitement brewing inside. A tough-looking Honda 480 dirt bike is sitting in the garage bay.

I fist bump Gabe, and we climb in the truck. Jaden's sprawled across the bottom bunk, already snoring.

"Did he sleep in here all night?" I ask.

"He didn't want to miss the bus," Slate says, sliding the truck into gear. "Team Taylor, welcome to the long haul."

My eyebrows go up. "I guess he *is* the dirt bike phantom."

The semi's engine soothes my mind as the miles pass until we reach the mountains. Then my thoughts lug down as we gain altitude and the landscape changes. It hits me that life is like that too. Sometimes there's a comfortable space where we can just cruise along, but sooner or later, there will be a mountain to conquer. That's when I realize how far I can go, how strong I really am.

"Anybody ready for a pit stop?" Slate asks.

I blink, wondering how long I was lost in thought. "Yeah, for sure."

Gabe and Jaden wrestle toward the fuel station doors, but I pause, gazing at the Taylor rig, knowing it's a miracle I belong to it.

A little boy slips past Gabe and Jaden as they enter the station, shouting. "Daddy! There's a race car in there!"

I turn with a grin as Slate strides up, stretching his shoulders. "Ah. We're living the dream, aren't we?"

I pull open the door for him, letting the knowledge settle deep. Team Taylor is my extended family, and I'd do anything to protect them. "Sure thing. Driving two thousand miles so we can race for three."

We laugh, but soon we're knocking more miles off that total. Jaden is on the top bunk, pitching tiny balls of straw wrappers down at Slate and Gabe. Deep in the rolling hills of Kentucky, I read a billboard that says, "The Corvette Museum, America's Sports Car."

"No way! Can we go?" Gabe asks, his face pressed against the glass.

Slate sighs, glancing at the GPS. "We still have a long way to go."

"I'm 'a freak out if I don't get out soon." Jaden's tone leaves no room for doubt. A paper ball bounces off Slate's head.

"Me too, bruh," he growls, and I catch his eye roll in the mirror.

Still, he pulls off at the exit, and my pulse spikes as I think about all the incredible cars we'll see. We hoot and holler as we leap from the semi before Slate puts it in park.

"Did you know that in the fifties, Chevrolet was in a slump?" Gabe asks as we step through the museum's front door. "They needed something new. It was code named Project Opal, and the first Corvettes had 3.9 liter straight-six engines. It took a while for the engines to catch on . . ."

We all turn, and our mouths fall open. Just beyond the lobby, shining cars fill our vision.

"But I'm so glad they did," Gabe whispers.

Slate catches up, and we buy tickets, then step into the rows of incredible cars. Each and every one is perfect, and some are so old, they must be worth millions.

"Hey, look, a bunch of these are on loan from private owners," Jaden says. "John should buy one and loan it to the museum for a while."

Gabe elbows me. "Yeah, but only if we don't get to it first."

I snort in agreement as I recall our mad dash escape in John's Ferrari, we had to take it off road and ended up totaling the car. I still can't believe I actually thought Gabe stole John's Ferrari. Slate flicks the brochure he's holding. "Here's where I want to go, the Corvette Cave-in."

Soon, we approach a big yellow sign.

"The Skydome Sinkhole Experience," I whisper.

The room has a high, arched roof and a ragged hole in the center of the floor. All around the vast hole sit wrecked Corvettes.

"Did a bomb go off in here?" Jaden asks.

"Just watch the video." Slate points to a massive screen that shows the same room in pristine condition.

The grainy security video holds steady on the cars. The blue Corvette on the left shifts just a bit. Then the entire concrete floor drops an inch. I gasp as the floor and the cars disappear in a massive cloud of dust. When it settles, the hole is all that's left.

"Oh, man," Gabe says, scanning the crushed cars that surround the hole. The hole is covered with clear fiberglass, but I don't trust what's below my feet anymore.

"Um," I say, clearing my throat, "how do we know there isn't another sinkhole under us?"

"I'm sure they did seismic tests to make sure before they reopened this exhibit," Slate says as he leans on the rail without concern. "But, you know, sometimes that happens inside a person too."

Jaden grips his chest, crumpling forward. "Ugh! There it is. All my cars caved in." He stands up straight.

Slate cuffs him on the back of the head. "What I meant was, you can never really tell what a person is made of until the pressure is on. Some people are hollow inside, spineless. Even if they have fancy things, big titles, and important positions, they don't hold up to the test of time."

I lean on the rail next to him, letting the thought settle in. "Guess you never know what's underground, do you?"

He looks over at me. "Nope. That's why you've got to keep your wits about you and watch out for that first shift. Sometimes that's all the warning you have that things are about to get crazy–one little twitch."

My thoughts fly as I stare at the hole. I sure hope this trip doesn't have any sinkholes. I need to win a race, and that takes complete focus.

By the time we leave the museum, having oohed and aahed over everything from classics to cars that aren't on the market yet, Slate's warning won't leave me. It settles like a boulder in my stomach as the miles zip by.

Only when the wide open space gives way to another set of mountains can I push the thought out of my mind. We play punch bug until our shoulders are sore, then we switch to seeing who can find the most dogs, before we start falling asleep out of boredom.

The miles pass as the days creep by. The landscape changes, drying out as we draw closer to LA. Hauling through the Mojave Desert is unnerving, with so many miles of nothing but sand, scrubby plants, and killer heat.

Slate grimaces as we top a mountain pass, revealing a sweeping view of LA. "Almost there. Just one last steep grade to conquer." My muscles feel tight after sitting still for so many days.

Two hours later, Slate pulls into Irwindale Speedway. The track is my world, even 2,000 miles from home.

"It's got one track inside the other," Jaden says, pointing to the double ovals.

"The inner one is one third of a mile, and the other is half a mile," Slate says. "We made good time, so after we unload, y'all can relax at the hotel—if Logan's parents can handle all of you."

We set up in pit row, helping Gabe set the camber for the half-mile track and double-checking that 77 made the trip safe and sound.

Gabe pulls out a small radio. "Look, I got a scanner. Now I can hear all the other teams during the race. It could come in handy."

"No cap?" Jaden asks, taking it from him and fiddling with the knobs. "It'll pick up the police radios too!"

Mom and Dad pull up in a rental SUV and whisk

us away into the city. We stare at the sights, and the sprawling vibe of LA seeps into us. We grab sandwiches called "French dip," invented right there in LA. Mom also gets each of us a one-tap bus ticket so we can get around LA on our own. We drive down the strip, looking at the lights. Then the three of us begin wrestling in the backseat.

"Okay," Mom says, "it's time to let you loose in the pool."

The hotel pool is gorgeous. Part of it is outside, and part of it is inside. I can't wait to dive underneath the barrier between the two.

"Now this is living!" Jaden yells as he jumps in.

Mom shows up later, but she's not in a bathing suit. "Logan, is your dad here with you guys?"

"No, we haven't seen him since we got here," I reply, splashing Gabe.

She scowls. "Okay, I'm going to the room to look for him."

By the time we're all back at the hotel room and in dry clothes, Mom's pacing. "Logan, I think your dad is missing."

– 9 –

"Missing? Why don't you call him?" I say.

"His phone's right there. He went for ice an hour ago. He never came back. I thought maybe he went down to check on you boys." She hugs herself, her face pale. "His wallet is here, and so are the car keys. I checked in the lot. The car is still right where we parked it."

"Hang on," I say, stuttering. "He's got to be here somewhere."

She shrugs. "I checked the lobby, the exercise room, and the restaurant. None of the employees have seen him."

Her fingers tremble as she rubs her forehead. She seems a lot more upset than she should be.

"He's a grown man. I'm sure he's fine, Mom."

She looks up at the ceiling. "Logan . . ." she covers her mouth with one hand, "there are some things you don't know—"

"About why we moved to North Carolina," I say, finishing for her.

"Yes." She sits down, bracing her arms on the couch. "I think we need to call the police."

"What?" I ask. *I knew they hadn't told me everything, but this must be worse than anything I could have imagined.*

"You'd better sit down," she says.

Gabe and Jaden offer to step out so we can talk in private.

"No, you can stay. It's time the story came out," Mom says. "Obviously, hiding it is no longer possible."

I perch on the end of a chair, my muscles like steel, every molecule focused on her.

She keeps rubbing her forehead. "Last October your dad took a case. It was all very low-key because the person he was defending didn't want it made public. That's happened plenty of times. He won, as usual. But the person who committed the crime is the brother of a powerful man."

"I take it he's not powerful in a *good* way," I say, my throat constricting.

"That's right, and Ikov Harding took it as an insult that Dad dared to convict a member of his family. We received some . . . *things* that made us very uncomfortable. We took every legal action, but we decided the only way to be safe was to move, to disappear until he let go of the grudge."

I sit back in the chair, studying the ceiling. My thoughts are racing at a million RPM. "So we were running."

"These people weren't kidding around, Logan. Our first priority was to protect you. But they must have been watching the flight lists. We should've thought about your dad's real name being on there. This is the first time he's flown since the move."

"But he uses his real name in North Carolina," I protest.

She shakes her head. "You probably never noticed, but we changed the law firm's name when we moved. Plus, the house is technically owned by the firm, and so are our cars. We've been fairly invisible."

She looks at the clock. "I can't wait any longer. I'm calling 911."

She moves into the bathroom to place the call,

still trying to shield me.

"Come on, let's go check the ice machines," Gabe says, his eyes glittering.

I feel like a gas engine burning diesel fuel. I'm not even sure I can move. *Dad's missing?*

Gabe grabs my hand and yanks me up, but my muscles are like water. We stride down the hotel hallway. Everything seems surreal, as if I'm watching someone else's life.

"Look," Gabe whispers.

A free taco punch card for Loco Taco is lying next to an ice bucket, which is tipped over onto its side.

Jaden's voice is low, "Yo. They were watching you in NC, too."

- 10 -

We return to the hotel room and lay out our theory and evidence for the police, who don't seem all that interested in *anything* we have to say.

"We just *can't* file a missing persons report yet. There's no *real* evidence of foul play, and I'm not going to cry wolf for you," the police officer tells my mom.

"What do you mean 'cry wolf'?" my mom nearly shouts. "My husband would never just disappear like this, and we just gave you proof that my husband was being followed all the way back in North Carolina!"

"Ma'am, if you want us to take you seriously, you need to settle down."

"I don't think the police are taking this seriously enough," Gabe whispers as the officer shakes his head before turning away from my mom to talk to his partner.

"It's the same thing we ran into in Iowa," Mom whispers back, turning toward us as the police officers start up a conversation. "The police are either incompetent, or they are being paid off by Ikov."

We all fall silent as the implications become obvious: if we can't trust the police, how will we save Dad?

I flinch at a crisp knock on the door. One of the officers opens it. Slate and John stand waiting outside. After identifying themselves, the officer lets them in. I feel better having them there, but their presence also ramps up the reality of the situation.

John steps toward my mom. "Whatever we can do, we're here for you, Mrs. Reed."

Mom blinks back tears, and I bite my tongue as I pull Slate aside and fill him in, stressing the Loco Taco card part and hinting that we might not get real help from the officers.

His blue eyes widen, and he nods as the pieces fall into place. "Let's take a look at the ice machine."

We march down the hallway like an army platoon. When we reach the ice machine, I take out my phone and start snapping photos of the scene, grabbing images from every angle.

Gabe and I frown at each other as Slate crosses his arms. "Mrs. Reed said your dad left to get ice," Slate says. "It seems fairly obvious that whatever happened, happened right here, yet the police don't seem very interested in setting up a crime scene . . ."

My brain races. Every second that ticks past makes it harder to find Dad. I motion to Gabe, Slate, and Jaden, and we move a bit further down the hall, away from the police officers outside of my parents' hotel room. It's going to be up to us to find him. The weight of it settles hard inside.

"We have to do something!" I cry, heart in my throat.

"We can't interfere with their investigation," Slate says.

"At this rate, we would be half a mile ahead of them and not in their way at all!" I insist, my hands clenched.

"We're sure of one thing that the cops aren't. Your dad *was* being watched in North Carolina too. The taco wrappers and punch card prove that much," Gabe adds, the intensity in his eyes making me so glad he's there.

"Hey," Jaden says, "I snapped some shots of that car near your place. I knew something was sus when I saw the way it was parked. No reason for a car to be there."

"You did?" My voice cracks, just like the last shreds of my cool.

"Yep." He scowls at his phone as he scrolls through images. "Here, this is a good one."

I snatch his phone and study a photo of the Camry with a great view of the interior and the passenger seat littered with papers.

Slate leans over my shoulder. "Zoom in on those papers."

"The top one is a car rental agreement," I say, squinting at it. Too bad I can't see the name at the bottom since it's under another sheet of paper.

"Makes sense," Slate replies. "They must have rented a car to follow us since they aren't from North Carolina. But look at that, the address on that other envelope shows a P.O. box in LA. They must have a base nearby.

"What are the chances we'd head right toward them?" Gabe asks, leaning in to look closer at the image. "Hey, what's that? Chop it Cycles?"

I zoom in further, but the finer print on the

body of the paper blurs. "I can't read anything except the name of the shop."

"Jaden, text this photo to all of us, will you?" Slate says. "We have to get it to the officers as well."

"Then what?" I ask, my heart slamming against my chest as I think of sitting there, waiting.

Slate sighs. "I don't suppose it would hurt to do a little . . . research."

"Yes!" Gabe says.

I bite the inside of my cheek, holding back a flood of emotions.

We burst into the hotel room like a football team. The officers are busy with paperwork, so I pull Mom aside.

"Can we head out to the city? Slate will take us in the rental." She shakes her head. "Mom, I can't just sit here and do nothing, you can call us if the police find anything and we will come pick you up."

"Logan, no. Please be patient. The police are working on it and I'm sure they aren't *all* untrustworthy. Plus, I couldn't risk losing you too." She clamps a hand over her mouth, tears pooling in her eyes as she fights the truth.

"Mom, you know we can't just sit around and do nothing."

Deep inside, a spark of determination flares into a furnace. I have to fix this. I have to do *something*.

I gesture toward Slate. "Slate will be with us, Mom. I mean, look at him. He's practically an entire team of bodyguards."

Slate is without a doubt the most muscular person in the room. Actually, in *most* rooms Slate would be the strongest.

She bites her lip, sniffing. "Let me ask the officers. Give me a minute."

She talks to a detective, then returns. "They're fine with you going out. I will wait to share your lead with them though, because I don't know who we can trust. I'll give you guys a fifteen minute lead, hopefully I'm wrong and the police will be right behind you, but I wouldn't hold your breath."

"See?" I whisper. "You know Dad would never leave without telling us. We have a good lead to follow, and we'll keep you posted."

She sighs. "Okay, but stick with Slate. He'll keep me posted about where you are, and make sure you're—"

"Being careful. Yeah, Mom. We will."

Before we leave, we notice a sudden commotion among the officers as one of them sets up a laptop on the small end table. We all crowd around to watch the security footage of the hallway. It's black and white, but the video is clear. People meander back and forth, some lugging bags. The air in the room grows tense. Then a tall man in a suit strides under the camera.

"It's Dad!"

Then the video flickers, and Dad's gone. Only the empty hallway remains. I scowl at the footage. The video goes blank again. Then we see the punch card and the ice bucket lying where Dad had just been.

I clench my fists, my lungs heaving. Mom lets out a shuddering breath.

"I'll try and track down the security footage. Maybe they have a backup somewhere," John says, pulling out his phone. "The rest of you can keep searching without me. I'll be in touch if I find anything."

Mom turns to me. "Go, Logan. Go find your dad."

- 11 -

"Chop it Cycles," Slate says as he parallel parks my parents' rental car in the tight space in front of the shop, which is nestled on a busy LA street.

Jaden pulls out a pair of earbuds, then sets the scanner down. "There's still no chatter on the police channels about your dad. I think we're his only hope."

I suppress a shiver of dread.

"Hang on," Gabe says. He's been working on his phone. "I put Jaden's photo through an editing program, which made the paperwork clearer. I even got the part number."

Slate nods, searching for a scrap of paper to write it on. "Here's the deal. We're a race team . . ."

Jaden blinks rapidly. "No kidding."

Slate frowns. "We have a race bike we need a part for. But we'll just let it play out and see what we learn."

I get out of the rental car, trying not to hyperventilate. I bend forward, putting my hands on my knees.

Slate's hand is on my shoulder. "Logan?"

I nod, but I can't form words. *Where's Dad? Will I ever see him again?*

"Come on. Let's go find him," Slate says.

The dizzy feeling subsides, and I follow Team Taylor into Chop it Cycles.

Slate strides up to the counter as I look at the showroom, which is full of chrome bikes with high handlebars.

"I got a part that came in . . ." Slate repeats the number as I lean on the counter. Under its clear plastic top, papers and business cards fill the space. One catches my eye: Chop it Cycles' annual legend car sale.

I elbow Slate and tap the spot. He scowls at it as the man searches for the part number. Slate's eyes dart back and forth as he nods.

"Okay . . ." The employee's name tag reads Brad. "Someone has already picked up that part."

"Really?" Slate says, shaking his head. "Does it say who got it? Maybe one of the guys on the team misplaced it."

Brad's eyes scan Slate's sharp-looking Team Taylor shirt. "Looks like a fellow named Gunnar picked it up two days ago."

Slate nods with a frown, as if he would expect Gunnar to lose a part. "'Course."

"Y'all must be racing legend cars, right?" Brad says. "Gunnar bought four of them just three months ago from our used showroom. That part was for 44. Are you racing that car?"

Slate laughs. "Not without that part!"

"True. Say, two more legend cars just came in. You want to take a look?"

Slate turns, pumping his eyebrows at us. Then we follow Brad through another door.

The cars glisten under the brilliant lights.

"Now, this one is a twin to 44. Same year, same upgrades," Brad says, lifting off the hood. The Yamaha motorcycle engine is pristine.

Thoughts zoom through my head like cars on a fast track. Is everything connected to racing somehow? Does Ikov own a race team? If so, how does racing lead to Dad?

Slate and Gabe chat about the cars as if it's all we have to do. Then Slate chuckles. "I think I can still smell Gunnar's tacos in here."

Brad laughs. "The man is never without them. The bag he had last time was still steaming. After work I hurried down there because I couldn't stop thinking about them."

I freeze, my eyes wide. Loco Taco is *here?*

"Well," Slate says, "I think we better find that stator Gunnar lost."

Brad grins. "I can always order another."

We file out, my fingertips tingling. As soon as the door closes, I'm on Slate. "How did you know it was a stator?"

He shrugs. "Stators produce electricity, and it's usually the first thing to go bad on a legend car."

As we pile into the rental car, Gabe points to his phone. "Loco Taco is less than a mile from here."

"Plus, we have a name, even if it's only a nickname," Slate says as he pulls into the heavy LA traffic. I scan the thick stream of pedestrians. Any one of them could be Gunnar.

We pass a tiny shop with a cartoon mouse holding up a taco on the sign. Loco Taco. We end up having to park almost a quarter mile away.

"Anybody hungry?" Slate asks as he gets out.

I open the door, then slam it as a city bus roars past less than an inch away. The close call tilts my nerves further toward freaking out. But the scent of tacos flowing down the street settles my stomach. Despite everything that's happening, I realize I'm starving.

We ford our way upstream through the crowd, and Gabe strides up to the Hispanic employee, firing away in Spanish. Seconds later, a massive tray of tacos is in his hands as we wander to one of the four small tables in the tiny dining area.

I pull my hoodie sleeves up as Jaden snatches

a taco, inhaling it before the rest of us can even sit down.

"Yum!" His eye roll says it all. "These are premium!"

He's right. Plus, I feel a bit more solid with some fuel in the tank. The taco place fills until people are lined out the door. Production slows down under the strain, and there's hardly room to stand inside.

"I can see why Gunnar loves 'em," Slate says around a mouthful.

The tray empties at an alarming rate.

"What did you say to him?" I ask Gabe.

He shrugs. "Nothing much. Should I get back in line and drop Gunnar's name?"

We all frown at the last taco. Jaden snatches it with zero remorse.

Slate draws a breath to speak, but one word echoes over the crowd, keeping us all silent.

"Gunnar!"

- 12 -

I freeze with my back to the counter. A piece of lettuce dangles from one side of Jaden's mouth as he stares at the scene behind me.

"Last time I saw you, you ordered two hundred tacos. Did you eat them all?" The man's thick Hispanic lilt makes me scowl as I try to decipher the words.

"Yeah, yeah. They were pretty stale by the end, but they got me through my trip," a deep voice says.

My hands clench in my lap. *Your trip to spy on my family!*

As my eyes fix on Slate's Team Taylor shirt, a jolt of adrenaline flows through me. "Slate," I hiss, "he'll see your shirt." Then I flinch. "He'll recognize every one of us!"

We stare wide-eyed at each other.

"Hit the bathrooms, quick!" Slate says, pushing back his chair.

I pull my hood up and keep my head low as we inch through the waiting crowd. The bathroom has just one stall and one urinal along the wall.

"We gotta follow him!" Gabe whispers. "If we lose him, we're done." He inches the open door, peering out into the restaurant. "Oh, man! He's coming!"

We all flinch, trapped inside the tiny room.

"Into the stall!" Slate shoves us forward. Jaden leaps onto the toilet seat, but the other three of us can't shut the door around our bulk.

"Hurry!" Slate is like a bull behind us as he shoves us in like sardines. I join Jaden, balancing on half of the narrow toilet seat. We both duck so our heads won't show above the half wall.

The door flies open, and we freeze, mashed together, trying not to breathe. I hope Gunnar won't notice the two sets of feet on the floor in one stall. His footsteps shuffle toward the urinal as he whistles a merry tune.

It turns my stomach, and I lose my balance, elbowing Slate in the neck. He scowls at me.

The door opens again, and the whistle fades.

"Go! Go! Go!" I urge.

We file out in time to see a tall man snatch a bulging bag of tacos from the counter and stride out.

"That's him!" Jaden weaves through the crowd like a wisp of smoke. I shoulder my way through. A moment later, Jaden is in the crowded street, pointing. "We're losing him!"

We jog through the crowd, zeroing in on Gunnar's black T-shirt and shiny bald head.

Slate puts his phone to his ear. "John, I think we're onto something here. It's time to make that call."

"What call?" I ask once he hangs up.

"John's got a buddy in the FBI. He's stationed here in LA."

I nod, so thankful for Team Taylor.

"Now I have to call this in to the detectives as well," Slate says. "Jaden, you and I will cross the street in case he turns."

As they veer over, Slate's voice gets lost in the crowd. "Officer Haley? We have a lead . . ."

Gabe and I push forward until we're right behind Gunnar. Fear and anger war inside me. Half of me wants to leap on him and demand my dad's location, but the other part recoils.

Gunnar crosses the street, and a girl on a skateboard has to swerve to avoid him, nearly losing her balance.

"Hey, I got tacos here!" he yells as she rolls past.

Thoughts of Piper and her most recent skateboarding competition flood my mind. Skateboarders are so athletic and nimble—just like Jaden. Maybe Piper would make a good addition to our team. We could use another person with Jaden's speed and athleticism. I snap out of it when we catch up to Slate and Jaden. Now isn't the time. I can bring it up later.

We group up and hang back, ensuring that Slate's phone conversation won't be overheard. Gunnar weaves across streets, going with the flow of the pedestrians instead of being hindered by them like us. I can tell he's lived here for a long time.

When Gunnar looks left, I motion for Slate to cross, but Gunnar doesn't turn. He jogs forward instead, racing for a packed city bus whose doors are closing.

"Hold up!" Gunnar shouts. A tall sign reads "Metro Bus, Silver Line J."

Gabe and I grimace as we slip through the doors right behind Gunnar. His taco bag slams against the yellow handrail inside the bus and splits open. He stops, scrambling to keep his food from spilling out.

Gabe shoves me past Gunnar, but almost all the seats are full. I shuffle toward the back as the bus lurches forward. The huge rear window gives me a clear view of Slate and Jaden running after us. Slate stops, out of breath, his arms held up in frustration.

"Sit down." Gabe prods me in the ribs. I slide in toward the window in the back row. A wild pattern of rainbow colors covers each seat.

I pull my hood lower as Gunnar comes our way, clutching the tacos against his chest. Gabe pulls his own hood up, and we slouch, our phones front and center.

With a sigh, Gunnar sits in the only available seat, right next to Gabe. Gabe stares at his phone, his face a shade paler than normal. His thumb hovers over the lock screen, doing nothing, so I elbow him.

He flinches when Gunnar takes out a taco, slurping and crunching. Gabe opens a racing game and promptly loses as Gunnar licks his fingers. I wince at the disgusting sound as the bus stops. I shift away so Gunnar can't see my face. The hair on my arms is standing on end as he chomps into another taco.

Five stops later, Gunnar brushes shredded lettuce off his shirt and then stands up. We hesitate, giving him space, then follow him off the bus.

The sign outside says "Union Station," but there's no time to sightsee. Gunnar is moving fast, cutting through the crowd.

My phone rings. It's Slate. "Where are you?" he asks, his voice tight with worry.

"Union Station," I whisper. "Hang on."

Gabe and I jaywalk, sprinting as Gunnar cuts behind the Hall of Records and strides up to a tiny shelter under the shade of some trees. "He's at 222 North Hill. There's a set of elevators!"

Gabe and I leap behind some bushes, groaning as we hit the ground. Once he's inside the elevator, Gunnar turns, scanning the quiet walkway.

The call disconnects, and I jam my phone into my pocket as the doors inch shut.

As soon as they close, we hurry forward. The building is nothing more than two elevator doors with a roof overhead.

One of the rusty steel doors has caution tape across it in an X and a sign that reads "Out of order."

The "down" button on the working elevator

goes dim. It's empty now.

Gabe looks at me. "Do it."

I nod and then push the button.

− 13 −

The button lights up, and the door creaks open, jamming halfway, then screeching open. Now the building looks like someone with a front tooth knocked out.

I glance at Gabe. He shrugs and then steps inside. I'm right behind him. The door struggles to close.

"Um . . ." I mutter, pressing the "down" arrow inside. It doesn't respond. I pull out my phone, but there's no cell signal.

Gabe looks around the tiny space, dirt and rust edging every corner. "Are we trapped in here?"

I hold my breath, listening hard.

The elevator shudders, and I brace against the wall. We drop an inch, then begin a torturous descent.

When the door finally opens, my shoulders relax. We ease into a concrete room with doors at either end. Garbage and dirt cover the floor.

A taco wrapper to the right draws us forward. Gabe pushes the gray steel doors open and scans the long concrete hallway. A sign on the wall says "Hall of Public Records."

I peer into the room, finding it full of metal cabinets and newspaper clippings. Ahead is an escalator. It's not running, so we jog up the stairs into another hallway. It's far older, with chunks of concrete missing. Ancient wooden doors block the way ahead, and a steep-angled tube cuts up into the wall. A powerful flow of air is blowing from it.

Clunk.

We freeze. A footstep on the escalator! Gabe and I slam into each other, scrambling to maintain our balance.

"Go! Into the tube!" he hisses.

There's nowhere else to hide, so I leap into the giant tube, only to slide back out.

"It's too steep!" I whisper.

Clank. Clunk.

"Go!" Gabe shoves me harder.

I scramble in again, forcing my back against the roof as my shoes slip. Gabe rams me like a bulldozer, forcing me higher. I spread out, my muscles trembling, and stick by sheer will.

"Go higher!" He smashes against me, his shoes somehow gripping the concrete tube.

"Can't," I grunt.

"Shh."

We freeze, holding our breath against the strong wind created by the ventilation system. The thud of footsteps draws closer. Seconds tick past, each one making me thankful for Slate's pit stop training program, which allows me to hold that tortuous position. The wooden doors at the far end of the hall creak, leaving behind only the fan noise.

The sharp crinkle of a paper wrapper makes me flinch, and I almost slip. He's still there, eating tacos. I grimace, and one foot slips an inch, hitting Gabe's shoe.

Gabe grunts as he begins to slip. Then the wooden doors creak again. I lose it, pile driving into Gabe, and we tumble in a heap on the concrete. Everything is silent.

Suddenly, an engine flares to life! Gabe is wide-eyed, listening. "That's a Yamaha FZ09."

"Of course you'd know it just by the sound," I say, easing off the floor. Vibrations from the engine rattle my hand when I place it on the wooden door. The engine revs higher, reverberating, then the sound grows faint.

"He's gone," Gabe says, slipping through the doors. Tire marks line the old stone tunnel, lots of marks, with the wheel bases close together.

"He's driving a legend car!" Gabe says, eyeing the streaks on the stone. This older tunnel is far smaller than the other hallway and round. It's barely as tall as I am. I pull out my phone and shine

its flashlight ahead.

"If we hurry, we can follow the scent of his exhaust," Gabe says, already trotting away.

I look back, trying to lock in some sense of direction before running after Gabe. Within a few steps, we come across an incredible piece of artwork. It's graffiti, just spray paint, but it looks like a giant raven spreading its wings, flying down the tunnel overhead.

I look at my phone screen and realize my phone is almost dead.

"Gabe," I whisper, "we only have a few minutes of light left."

The darkness of the tunnel behind us makes me shiver. Gabe swallows hard, a sheen of sweat on his brow. In that second of complete silence, a snatch of a voice reaches us. We crouch.

"Turn it off!" Gabe says, covering my phone with his hand.

– 14 –

We wait in the pitch dark. As my eyes adjust, however, I see a slim bar of light in the tunnel far ahead.

"I smell . . . tacos," Gabe whispers.

"Dad must be here." I slip the phone into my pocket and inch forward.

"You forgot the ice?" A deep voice says, making my skin crawl.

"Sorry, Vinn. I'll get it next time," Gunnar replies.

"That's what you said last time," Vinn says.

I jut my chin toward a room on our right that houses three legend cars. Gabe studies them as the voices resume.

"When will the boss be here? I want my pay for bringing Mr. Fancy Pants in."

Gabe and I share a sharp glance. I grit my teeth. There's no way I'm leaving without Dad.

The tunnel had plenty of other spots where rooms branched off, but they all appeared to be empty.

I creep next to the first door. It's different from the others. It's metal, and it's definitely a new addition. There's a big lock with a digital keypad pad to open it.

I tilt my head. Another engine roars deep inside the tunnel!

"Hey, Ikov's coming. Go check on our guest."

There's a sudden shuffle inside the room. Gabe and I scramble to hide. I leap behind one of the legend cars. The door opens, and light fills the stone chamber.

Gabe lands hard on his side behind another car, his head mashed against its rear tire. The squeak of a metal hinge makes my blood curdle. Despite the growing noise of the engine, I can still hear footsteps.

"Yeah, he's just sitting there, staring at the door. It's creeping me out."

"Hush up, Gunnar. The boss will be here in a minute, and he doesn't like garbage lying around. Clean this place up."

The motor drowns out the familiar crinkle of taco wrappers as headlights shine down the tunnel.

I curl further behind a tiny car as another car, with 44 painted in bright blue on its side, pulls up. The driver gets out and strides over toward the other men.

"We need a distraction," I whisper, my eyes darting down the tunnel as the door shuts, cutting off the light.

"Let's push this car farther down," Gabe says, his eyes gleaming in the dimness. At that moment, I realize I wouldn't want to be in this tight spot with anybody else.

"Right."

We rush forward. Pushing the car is so familiar, as if it's just another day at the track. We tiptoe past the double doors. I study the second door. Dad is right behind it.

The door is made of dull gray metal with an ordinary keyhole lock. It has a small flip-down window for mail delivery, just a few inches wide.

We push harder, the tires creaking on the cement. Then we pass another room. It's empty except for a few cases of water, a fuel can, and some motor oil.

"Stop it here," Gabe says. "We'll hide in that room. When they come to check this out, we'll slip back and get your dad." His confidence is contagious.

"What are you going to do?" I ask.

"Let's turn it sideways!"

There's not a second to lose. It takes all the muscle we have to shove the rear end sideways so it's blocking the tunnel. Now the legend car looks like a hamster in a wheel.

"Go get the motor oil. Hurry!" Gabe hisses, leaning into the tiny car.

A few heartbeats later, I'm back, holding the jug.

"Pour it all over the wall!" he says as he wraps something around the car's gas pedal.

"Right," I whisper, splashing the thick amber oil over the wall. It runs down, cascading over the front tires.

Gabe crouches next to me in the dark, his heavy breathing filling the air.

"Once I start this car, we rush for the supply room. When the guys pass us, we sneak back to your dad. I'll get the other cars ready while you get him out."

I nod, though a million questions are piling up in my mind. Gabe's plan has as many holes in it as an oil filter. I open my mouth, but Gabe is already twisting, reaching for the start button.

"Go!" he growls, and the engine screams to life. The car's lights flicker on, and the tires spin, forcing the car to ride up the wall. I sprint toward the supply room as the rubber zings on the slick oil.

I slam through the supply room door, Gabe right behind me. We hold our breath as shouts erupt and footsteps pound down the tunnel. Three men sprint past our door.

Gabe and I peel out, jamming together in the doorway.

Ahead, the tunnel is full of light. They left the first door open!

Shouts merge with the screaming engine behind me as I veer into the room where the men had been waiting. A table is in the center with a plate of half-eaten tacos on it. A couch and a filing cabinet take up the rest of the small space. The table with the remains of tacos is littered with papers and soda cans. I sweep one arm across, and a metallic screech causes hope to surge up. It sounds like keys!

The keyring flies off the far end of the table and slides under the couch. I dive after the keys, landing hard on my stomach. My fingers sift through dust balls and other unidentifiable objects.

There!

I grip the keychain, my shoes peeling out as I scramble away. I skid in front of Dad's door, fumbling with the keys.

Chaos echoes in the tunnel, and I feel exposed standing in the light.

"Come on!" I hiss, jamming a key into the slot. It doesn't fit! Five tries later, one slides home. I twist it, ramming the door open.

There's a roar in the dark.

The sound makes me freeze. Someone is racing toward me—then I'm crushed against the wall!

"Dad!" I squeak as his shoulder drives into my stomach. "Dad, it's me!"

The pressure lets up as Dad's voice fills my ears. "Logan? They got you too?"

I grab his arm, trying to reinflate my lungs. "No! We're busting you out of here!"

Another engine flares to life. Gabe!

"Hey!" someone shouts from down the hall.

"Go!" I shove Dad through the open door, his tie flapping over one shoulder.

Gabe is pushing the second car into the tunnel.

"They're coming," I yell, pushing Dad forward.

Gabe sends a horrified glance down the shaft. Then he pushes the second car toward the men who are sprinting after us.

"Watch out!" he shouts as we sprint past the car. He wedges the half-empty oil bottle against the gas pedal, then starts the car. It shoots forward, careening down the tunnel like a bowling ball.

I look at the two remaining cars. They're so small, with only room for one person each. Gabe leaps into the other car, which is still backed into its spot.

"It won't start!" he yells.

Shouts reverberate down the tunnel as one of the goons gets past the speeding legend car.

"There's no time!" I shout. "Everybody in!" As we rush for the remaining car, Dad pushes me toward the door. "You'd better drive, Logan. We'll hold on!"

I scrunch inside, my hands on the wheel. The car rocks as Gabe contorts through the rear window, his legs hanging out the back. "Ouch!"

Dad rests his chest on the roof, balancing on the narrow rear bumper. "Go!"

I floor it.

The Yamaha motorcycle engine screams, overloaded with the three of us. A glance in the rearview mirror makes me press the paddle even harder. Gunnar is almost on top of us!

A tremendous crash comes from behind. I assume our two sabotaged cars have met.

My eyes are glued to the side mirror as I urge the tiny car forward. As we gain speed, Gabe grunts in my ear, his legs dangling behind the car. The wheels finally find traction, leaving Gunnar behind.

I shift through the gears, then reach up and pat Dad's hand, which grips the roof right above my head. "We got you, Pops!"

His wild laugh makes me grin. But then headlights flash behind us, and my grin disappears. "Gabe? I thought the other car wouldn't start!"

He grimaces, twisting to look. "It wouldn't! He must've known a trick to start it. We have to stop him. We can't outrun him overloaded like this."

"How?" I bellow as we zoom down the tunnel. An intersection in the shape of a Y appears ahead.

"Which way?" I yell.

"Um . . ." Gabe grunts.

"I don't remember there being a second tunnel!"

"Me neither!" he shouts.

I swerve with just seconds to decide.

"Left, go left!" Dad says.

The fender crunches against the wall as I cut left. The car resettles inside the new tunnel.

"Uh-oh!"

- 15 -

Ahead, the narrow tunnel floor shimmers in the headlights.

"Ah!" I shout. The legend lurches as it hits the water, sending spray straight to the ceiling.

The resistance forces us to swerve, swinging up one side of the tunnel and then the other. I wrestle the wheel as our weight forces us higher up the wall with each swerve. I downshift, and our reduced speed drops us back to the ground.

Dad pounds the roof. "Hurry!"

Headlights glare in the rearview mirror. They're right behind us!

"Any brilliant ideas?" I shout as I nail the gas, gripping the steering wheel as we cut through the water like a sailboat.

"Take the right!" Dad's shout is faint, and I almost miss it. Ahead, there's another split.

My stomach turns. We're getting lost fast, deep under the city of LA.

We lurch into the right-hand tunnel. Now out of the water, we make better speed, but the other car is still gaining!

"I have an idea!" Gabe says as he contorts like a snake, reaching out the passenger-side window with his feet still hanging out the back.He wrenches on the rear fender that's been flapping since I clipped the wall. He grunts as it loosens further, and sparks fly as it tings against the wall. Somehow, he forces it higher, and the sparks spread. Finally, he lets the fender go, and it clangs around behind us.

A satisfying crunch makes me whoop in victory.

"He hit it!" Dad shouts. "Ugh. He's still coming!"

I scowl at the rearview mirror. The goon's car is sparking like fireworks, our fender jammed under his front bumper.

"Logan, hit the other wall!" Gabe shouts, pulling his upper half back inside.

"Dad, watch out!" I shout as I veer toward a

doorway. The car jerks as the right fender makes contact and shears off the front bolts. Then it's like a sail, pulling the car hard to the left.

"Get it off there!" I scream as I fight to control the car.

Gabe shifts around my seat, inching out the back window as we speed down the tunnel. The front end feels loose. What if it's damaged too?

"Whoa!" I yell as the front tires come off the ground. My headlights are bouncing off the ceiling. "Gabe, get back in here!"

He vaults inside, and the car slams down, the fender still pulling us hard to the left.

"Go through the window!" I urge, watching Gunnar's headlights gaining behind us.

"Oh, sure," Gabe mutters as he contorts to the driver's window. The fender squeals, sparks shooting, and the dangerous pull ceases.

Crash!

"Whoo-hoo!" we shout as Gunnar falls back, his headlights fading.

"How do we get out of here?" I yell as we flash past ancient wooden doors and empty rooms.

"There's another tunnel. Go right!" Gabe points. One of his shoulders is on the tiny car's floor, and he's pinned between my seat and the door.

"Bad news, boys. He's back!" Dad shouts, still gripping the roof as headlights reappear behind.

I crank the wheel, ramping up the new tunnel.

"Hold up!" Gabe peers out the windshield, stretching as high as he can reach. "Dead end!"

A wall of solid concrete is straight ahead.

I brake hard, letting out a shout as the tires squeal. We slide to a stop half an inch from the wall. My chest heaves as I stare at the gray concrete.

"It's a T. Wait, look!" Gabe points right where a spray-painted raven spreads its wings in the tunnel.

"Yes!" I crank the wheel, the bumper squealing against the wall as Gunnar bears down on us. Shifting through the gears, we speed toward the wooden doors that lead to freedom.

In the rearview mirror, I see Gunnar's car still sparking as it slides through the sharp T, gaining precious seconds on us.

"He's right on our tail!" Gabe shouts in my ear.

"Duck, Dad!" I yell as we slam over the wooden door frame into the newer concrete tunnel.

"Don't slow down!" Dad shouts.

Ahead is the escalator that leads down to the elevator.

"Logan!" Dad bellows as I speed toward the escalator's waist-high handrails.

"Gabe!" I scream. "Get in the back!"

His eyes wide, he scrambles out the back window, and the front end lifts off the ground.

"Whoa!" we shout as the car slams into the wide rubber railings. Our speed tilts us forward, and we teeter as if on a playground toy. The front wheels are high in the air, spinning on nothing.

"Gabe, get back up here!"

He dives through the rear window, crumpling against the dash. The car groans, tilting forward. The wheels slam onto the handrails.

I pump the brakes, but the rubber just slides down the escalator's steep incline.

"Hold onto something!" I shout, as we careen toward the floor.

"Oomph!"

The front bumper crumples, and Dad slides onto the windshield as I rev the engine. We slam down to the flat. The elevator is just ahead, and the door is still stuck open!

"He's coming on foot!" Dad shouts as he scrambles back to the roof. His legs are blocking most of the windshield.

Parts are dragging everywhere as I aim straight for the elevator doors.

"We're not going to fit!" Gabe cries.

"Oh . . . yes . . . we . . . are!" I lock up the brakes as we flash inside, and the front bumper slams into the elevator's back wall.

"Push the button!" I scream.

The car fills every square inch of the elevator. I can't even open my door. Dad wiggles backward on the roof, one finger pounding the "up arrow" button.

"Hurry!" he shouts at the ancient elevator.

The door lurches, then creaks. Gunnar is sprinting down the hall, his bald head shining in the light. I grip the wheel, staring at him in the rearview mirror as he closes in.

"Go!" Dad yells at the stubborn door. He's still on the roof, yanking at the door as it sticks. At last it slides home with a final screech, and Gunnar slams into the other side.

"Going up," Dad whispers as the elevator gives an ominous screech.

Gabe tries to shift, but his rear end is pressed against the elevator door.

We lurch upward, then drop an inch.

"Come on, baby," I say, frozen in place.

The hydraulics whine, and we resume our snail's pace to the surface. The elevator rocks again, the ground-level button lighting up. The door jerks, and Gabe smashes forward, relieving the pressure. It squeals, opening an inch to reveal a platoon of officers with weapons drawn, FBI written in white letters on their uniforms. As the door creaks open, the rear bumper falls off with a clang.

"Mr. Reed?"

Slate's snapping pictures over the officers' shoulders as gravity pulls Gabe backwards, and he flops to the concrete floor.

"If you hurry, you'll catch Ikov and two of his employees down in the tunnels," Dad says, still lying on the roof.

By the time we get the car out of the elevator, Mom is there, hugging us all. She looks at the car. "I'm not sure I want to know what happened."

"You probably wouldn't believe it, anyway," I reply.

"Looks like you drove her pretty hard," Slate says as he eyes the car.

I turn to look. There's not much left. "Reminds me of Sophia."

Gabe laughs. "Just as long as you treat 77 better,

I'll be happy."

Jaden's sipping on a blue slushy. "Man! I missed all the action."

"Good thing too. I don't know where we would have stuffed you," I say, eyeing his drink. It looks good, but thoughts of the winner's circle and NASCAR banish my cravings.

"Hey, no junk food!" Slate says, swiping the drink from Jaden's hand. "We have a race tomorrow. We need to be in top shape!"

John strides up, rubbing his hands. "You all deserve a break. I'll cancel the race."

"No! I'm ready," I say. "This was a great warmup."

John adjusts his blue ball cap. "You sure? Are we all on the same page here?"

I look at the team, and they nod. "Yeah, we came here to conquer Irwindale. Let's get this done."

John smiles. "Now, that's a race team."

- 16 -

The next morning I roll out of bed, full of fire. I stand there watching Dad sleep. I never thought I'd be so glad to have him around.

At the breakfast bar, I ignore the waffles and do-nuts and fill my plate with eggs, bacon, and fruit. Slate nods, his tray looking just like mine.

Soon the smell of the track fills my nostrils, and I run one hand over 77's black hood in the red flare of sunrise.

"Ready, boy?" I ask, squatting next to him.

It's quiet so early in the morning, no engines screaming, but I can hear them in my soul.

"That's right. This track is ours." I set my hand on the racing slicks, the hours of pit-stop training making me thankful for a simple, dry track.

Soon the pits fill with teams as race time draws nearer. I try not to think about the man who'll be sitting in skybox twelve watching the race. We're not ready for NASCAR yet, but if I don't impress this guy, we might never be.

Jaden, Gabe, and I lean over 77's engine. Someone steps up next to me. I look up, expecting Slate. Instead, it's a scrawny guy with a scraggly beard and a black T-shirt. "This car slaps," he says, rubbing his beard. "Low key, though. I got some bussin' add-ons for you. It'll add thirty horsepower and win you this race."

We all turn to him, but it's Gabe who answers. "What you got?"

"A clip-on. Guaranteed no track inspector will find it. That's no cap. Plus, I already hooked up two other cars. So you don't stand a chance without this mod."

My stomach clenches as I glance at Gabe. This guy's talking about modifications that could get us banned from racing.

"Couldn't help overhearing you got a lot riding on this one," the man continues. "Just want to help my bros out."

My nerves spike as he stands there watching us. Then he shrugs. "I'll be around. It only takes sixty seconds to install. You can do it right after inspection, and nobody will know." He turns and walks off.

We stare at 77. I chew my lip, John's words rolling around in my head. Which way is better? Do we win no matter what?

"He's right," Jaden says. "Maybe a little help would be good. All I have to do is change tires. Winning this race is up to you guys. And it sounds like an 'L' would be bad right about now."

Gabe's mouth is tight as he runs his hand over 77's chrome valve cover. Crossing my arms, I scan the track. Dave's words come back to me: *The long road is the one worth traveling.*

Waiting to hear about whether or not I would lose my license after finding Sophia is still fresh inside too. I never want to be in that position again.

Gabe shakes his head. "Logan, it's your car. What do you think?"

I frown, clenching my jaw as I envision the two modified cars blowing past me. My eyes stray to box twelve. "If we ever get to NASCAR, it won't be because we cheated. I'm done with that. If we got caught, we'd be putting John and Slate on the chopping board, too. We have a team to protect because it's a *team* and not a modification that's gonna win races."

Gabe nods, a smile growing on his face. "Yeah, I agree." Then he studies the engine. "Let me see if I can eke out a little more horsepower."

"Sounds good. I'm going to need it." Being willing to lose is tough, especially with everything John has riding on this race. I need to remain honest, with the hope that the winds will be on my side.

"Should we tell somebody that some of the cars are modified?" Jaden asks, scowling down pit row.

"There's no way to know which ones or if the guy was even telling the truth," Gabe says as he tinkers with 77.

By the time evening rolls around, I'm a ball of nerves. I'm stepping into my race suit when Dad walks into the semi-trailer and sits on a chrome toolbox.

"I'm sure glad to be here tonight." His voice breaks, and I turn to look at him. A sheen of tears makes his eyes gleam. "And that's thanks to you, Logan."

I can't think of anything to say, so I just shrug.

"My entire life I've focused on one thing—building the law firm to give you and Mom the life you dream of. So I'd have something to hand down to you someday. In Iowa, when all this started with *the* case, I realized maybe I've been doing it wrong. I tried to show you I love you by giving you things. But I missed a lot of other opportunities to make sure you *know* it."

He laughs, his eyes filled with a far-off look. "When you showed up in that tunnel, I thought they had caught you too. Right then I realized how proud I am of you, win or lose, pass or fail. I'm so glad you're my son." He blinks, looking up at the roof. "I'm not really good with words unless it's in court."

He stands, his powerful arms pulling me into a hug. The stress melts away. Win or lose, my family and my team are right here, rooting for me.

"I love you, son."

"Love you too, Dad."

He nods. "I wanted to tell you that Ikov's in jail, and I intend to keep him there. The police found piles of evidence in the tunnels, enough to convict him on loads of charges. We're safe now."

"Does that mean we're moving back to Iowa?" I ask. The thought turns my stomach.

"Well, it's a possibility. But moving across the

country isn't exactly easy. What do you think?"

"I . . . North Carolina is home now." It's all I can get out past the sudden tension in my chest.

"Well, I'm glad to hear that because I think it's the right place for us too."

I let out a breath. "Me too." Then I laugh, light flooding my soul. "Ikov messed with the wrong attorney."

"You bet he did. Hey, drive like you did in that tunnel, and you'll beat every car out there tonight."

I smile. "Number 77 is a far cry from a legend packed like a clown car."

"That's right," he says as he walks out. "Tonight you'll fly."

When he's gone, I let out a sigh. All the pressure lifts, and just one thing is burning in my heart.

Drive.

I zip up my suit, tuck my helmet under one arm, then stride out to 77. I hop in and slip on my fire-proof helmet sock, then the thin fireproof sleeve, and then buckle into the five-point harness.

Slate leans in the window. "Got a new HANS device. It's state-of-the-art, guaranteed to protect your neck." He slides the neck restraint and pro-tector under the seatbelt's shoulder straps.

"Fancy," I say.

Slate clips the HANS device onto my helmet and then slides the headrest pads between my head and the seat. "Good thing we won all that money," I say. "Now my noggin will be extra safe."

Slate laughs, tapping my helmet. As Piper would say, I'm protecting my greatest weapon.

I smile at the thought, wishing she were here. I pull on my gloves and do a radio check. Then I snap on the steering wheel. Each motion brings me closer to the race, sharpening my focus.

Slate pulls up the new window net, but Gabe shoulders his way in before he finishes clipping the net on.

"Hang on a second. Listen, I advanced the timing by two degrees. The engine will be hard to start, and it will idle rough. But at full throttle, it'll give you some extra punch. I won't leave the timing like that after this, but it'll be there when you need it tonight," Gabe assures me.

"Listen, boys, this race is two hundred miles," Slate says. "The tires are good for around one seventy; plus you'll need fuel. Depending on how stiff the competition is, we'll shave the fuel down to lighten the car. There's a balance and a risk between having just enough to finish and running out. We have a battle ahead, and Team Taylor plans to win. Working together is crucial."

I fist bump Gabe, then take a deep breath as Slate clips the net into place.

The announcer's voice rattles the air. "Start your engines!"

At the command, I press the ignition button. 77 grumbles, coughs, then falls silent.

My eyes go wide, and I glance at Gabe.

"It's alright!" he shouts over the other cars. "It'll start. Try again."

I smash the button again, and 77 cranks, its engine rumbling to life like an old muscle car.

The pace car leads us as we warm up our tires and get a feel for the track, but 77 is still running rough, its engine clanging along.

"Come on, boy. You just have to put up with it this one time."

My position is third, so I assume the two cars ahead of me are the ones with the modifications. The pole position is held by 29, and a bright red car with 98 on its side is straight ahead.

The pace car pulls off, and 77 presses me back

in the seat as the race begins. As I hit the accelerator, the engine smooths out just like Gabe said it would, and we ramp through the first turn.

"Alright Logan, you're in this for the long haul," Slate says over the radio. "We have plenty of time to move up. Trust the car, and let the track show you when to make a move."

I nod as 77 shimmies while coming out of turn four. There's a rough patch there. We whip out clean laps, the field stringing along as other drivers settle into a comfortable pace.

The laps condense into a mantra in my mind—rough spot, the extra tilt on to turn one, the slightest hump as we pass the pits. Time melts into another dimension where I exist solely to race.

Smoke billows up, and fenders go flying on the far side of the track as a caution flag snaps.

"Come in, Logan!" Slate says as all the cars pull into pit row.

"It's really early for this," Slate says as Jaden pops off the lug nuts. The *zzir, zzir, zzir* of the lug gun echoes in my ears. Half a heartbeat later, there's the slightly different sound of Jaden putting on the fresh tire. *Zzzrip, zzzrip!* As 77 rocks, they switch sides, and before I even get to ten, John's pulling the fuel tank away.

"You guys are on fire!" I yell as 77 slams flat and I take off on the count of nineteen.

"Uh-oh," Slate says over the radio, making me grip the wheel harder.

"What's going on?"

"We're going to be cutting it close on fuel down the stretch! Let me run some computer analysis before we decide if you'll need to pit stop again before the end."

I don't answer, too busy tucking 77 in front of 98. That speedy stop earned us second place, and I won't give it up easily!

Laps roar past, and we begin to pass the back markers, the field now a muddle of racers.

"He's coming up on the inside!" Slate's warning makes me swerve as I pass a white back marker, keeping just ahead of 98.

He's definitely got a power boost that I haven't faced before, and it takes all of my skill to fend him off.

I growl, hating that he's racing dirty. Still, I can't accuse him based on mere suspicion. That's for the track inspectors to figure out.

Heat builds until I'm slick with sweat. I shake

my head as it drips into my eyes. I focus on slowing my breathing to fend off heat-related stress. For the first time ever, I'm glad I skipped that soda.

"Alright, the computer's predicting you will have one eighteenth of a gallon of extra fuel. Running out is a sure way to lose. That's cutting it too close. You have to come in around lap four seventy."

I veer in front of 98's fourth attempt to pass. "Can't do that, Slate. These guys aren't joking around. If I'm light on my brakes, I can increase the fuel mileage. It'll buy me a couple hundred yards each lap."

"We have twenty laps to decide, but we can't be wrong," Slate warns.

I nod, finding an open place in the field with 29 out ahead. I ask a little more from 77, and I keep my bumper a few inches from 29's, letting the draft help me out, knowing that a fuel stop will mean losing.

"We got this," I whisper, easing off the accelerator to avoid using the brakes. I lose precious inches from 29, but I slingshot through the turn harder than before, grimacing as I grip the wheel, on the edge of control. The move lets me catch back up. This race is a game of sheer determination. I look for a caution flag, which would give us plenty of time, but it doesn't come.

"This is it, Logan. Only thirty laps left. What's your call?"

Slate's tone makes me grimace. If I make the wrong decision . . . but Dad's words push me forward: "Win or lose, I'm proud you're my son."

"Gotta trust the car, Slate. I think we got this."

He's quiet for half a lap, and my heart pounds as I zing around the steep banks. "Alright. It's possible you'll make it. But we don't know if the timing advance changed the fuel usage."

After two hours of intense racing, my arms are trembling, but I lock it down, drawing energy from deep inside. Fifteen clean laps later, we're all feeling the pressure, and drivers are pushing even harder.

I clench my jaw as 29 gains distance from me and forces me to use the accelerator harder. The risk of running out of gas hovers in my mind. Ten laps to go.

"Hold on. Gabe's got something on his scanner!" Slate's excitement ramps up my adrenaline, allowing a sharp focus to return through the exhaustion.

"Twenty nine is running hot! Get up there and bump him a little, Logan. Do it now!"

As 77 surges forward, the advanced timing

shines through. I hover on 29's bumper.

"Touch him just a tiny bit while he's distracted!" Slate urges. I grimace, putting the pedal to the floor. The contact is soft, but it shoves 29 higher into the turn. I back off and then dive into the narrow opening the move created.

"Yes!" I shout as 29 lets out a puff of smoke, then drops away as I surge around turn four.

"He's done. Car 29 is out with engine trouble. He's clear of the track, and there won't be a caution, Logan!" The tension in Slate's voice makes me grit my teeth.

I have eight laps to hang on to this victory.

When 98 rams me hard, I ride the contact without slowing, forcing 77 to hold to the racing line.

"Easy! Don't let them pass," Slate urges.

The g-forces tear at me as I drive hard, defending first place.

I blink, and the headlights in the tunnel come back in a rush. The sensation of pursuit spikes my focus as 98 and I sling into the last lap. He's wide on the turn and gaining on me! The white flag snaps overhead, and we're nose to nose!

"Two turns left!" Slate shouts as 98 and I duke it out.

Number 98 slams into me broadside as we barrel toward the finish line. Meanwhile 77 goes into a wild slide and won't respond to anything I do. Both cars are locked together as we enter a spin that gains speed.

The grandstands and the infield blur together as we careen down the track at full speed, but 77 coughs, sputters, and then falls silent. Out of gas!

I clench my teeth as we slow, the grade forcing us to the inside of the oval track. We grind to a halt as the rest of the field thunders by.

"Is it a DNF?" I ask, trying to breathe in the intense heat. A "did not finish" is the worst outcome I could imagine.

"Uh, hang on." Slate runs toward me, one hand pressing the radio into his ear. "Ha ha! You crossed the finish line backwards! Two wheels were over the line ahead of 98! Nice win, Logan!"

He slaps my shoulder as I get out, my muscles straining, feeling just as empty as 77's gas tank. Car 98's driver glares at us.

Gabe rushes forward. "Did you shut the engine off?"

"No, man. We ran out of gas under the checkered flag, going backwards!"

After Gabe, Slate, and Jaden work with 98's pit crew to pry the cars apart, we line up for pictures.

"Well, you've got your work cut out for you," I say to Gabe as we look over the crunched car body. Then we turn, standing on 77's good side and grinning as the cameras flash.

"We might put in a bigger fuel cell and maybe a reserve tank," Slate says, his mouth frozen in a smile for the photos.

John waves to a well-dressed man and then shakes his hand. "Logan, I'd like you to meet Mr. Peters."

I give him a firm handshake, knowing I gave the race everything I had and then some.

"You've got an impressive team, John," Mr. Peter says. "Never seen a finish quite like that one, but you could use at least one more member. Think about how fast your pit times could be."

As John and Mr. Peters wander back toward the skybox, I start thinking of potential new team members. I turn to the guys. "What do you think of having a girl on the Taylor pit crew?" I ask, the idea brewing in my mind.

"Cindy?" Gabe says, his eyes lighting up.

"I was actually thinking of Piper." But as a shadow crosses Gabe's face, I add, "We should talk about it some more. I'm open to ideas."

Slate crosses his arms. "I'm not sure we could handle that many hormones floating around. Hey, anybody hungry? How about a Loco Taco?"

We all groan as Slate grins, slapping me on the back.

Other Bakken Books Stories

Camping books for kids

Mystery books for kids

Hunting books for kids

Fishing books for kids

www.bakkenbooks.com

Math adventures for kids

History adventures for kids

Space adventures for kids

Humorous adventures for kids